Contents

THE SECRET GARDEN   4

BLACK BEAUTY   22

THE RAILWAY CHILDREN   40

THE WIND IN THE WILLOWS   58

ALICE IN WONDERLAND   76

The publishers would like to thank the following authors for their
abridgements of the full-length Classic stories: Joan Collins (Railway Children,
Wind in the Willows, Alice in Wonderland); Joyce Faraday (Secret Garden);
Betty Evans and Audrey Daly (Black Beauty).
The woodcuts were individually hand carved in box wood
by Jonathan Mercer.

Material used in this book was previously published as part of the
Ladybird Classics series.

Ladybird books are widely available, but in case of difficulty may be ordered by post or telephone from:
Ladybird Books – Cash Sales Department Littlegate Road Paignton Devon TQ3 3BE Telephone 01803 554761

A catalogue record for this book is available from the British Library

Published by Ladybird Books Ltd Loughborough Leicestershire UK
Ladybird Books Inc Auburn Maine 04210 USA

A
Treasury
of
Classic
Stories

Ladybird

The Secret Garden

by Frances Hodgson Burnett
illustrated by Gilly Marklew

Mary Lennox

Mary Lennox was a spoilt, rude and bad-tempered child. She was never really well, and she was thin, miserable and sour-faced. No one liked her at all.

None of this was really Mary's own fault. She was born in India, where her father worked. He was always busy with his work, and paid no attention to his daughter. Her mother cared only for parties and pleasure. She left Mary in the care of an Indian nursemaid, who gave the little girl everything she wanted so that she would not cry and upset her mother.

So, not surprisingly, Mary grew up into a spoilt and most unpleasant girl.

One hot morning, when Mary was nine years old, she had a strange feeling that something was wrong. From her room she heard shouts and cries and the patter of hurrying feet, but no one came to her. She lay back on her bed and fell asleep.

When she awoke, the house was silent. Still no one came to her, and Mary was angry. Suddenly the door opened, and two Englishmen came in.

'Why was I forgotten?' Mary asked, indignant. 'Why does nobody come?'

'Poor little kid,' said one of the men. 'There's nobody *left* to come.'

No one liked her at all

That was how Mary learned that her father and mother had been killed by a disease sweeping the country. The servants had died, too. Mary was alone. There was no one in India to look after her, so she was sent to England to live with her uncle, Mr Craven, at Misselthwaite Manor in Yorkshire.

In London, Mary was met by Mrs Medlock, her uncle's housekeeper. Mary disliked her at once. But then, Mary disliked everyone. As they travelled north, Mrs Medlock told Mary about the house. It sounded very grand and gloomy, and stood on the edge of a moor.

'There'll be nothing for you to do, and your uncle won't bother with you,' said Mrs Medlock. 'He was a sour young man until he married. His wife was very pretty, and he worshipped her. When she died, it made him more strange than ever. He's away most of the time, so you'll have to look after yourself.'

'What's the moor like?' asked Mary.

'It's just miles and miles of wild land,' replied Mrs Medlock sharply. 'Nothing lives on it but wild ponies and sheep.'

It was dark when they got out of the train. A carriage took them to the house, where a butler greeted them at a huge oak door. 'You're to take her to her room,' he told Mrs Medlock. 'The Master is going to London tomorrow, and he doesn't want to see her.'

Mary followed Mrs Medlock upstairs and through many corridors to a room with a fire burning and supper on the table. 'This is where you'll live,' she said to Mary. 'Just see you stay here and don't go poking round the rest of the house.'

This was Mary Lennox's welcome to Misselthwaite Manor. It made her feel cross and unwanted and lonely.

THE GARDENS

The next morning a housemaid came to Mary's room. She was called Martha, and she chatted as she worked.

Mary was not used to friendly servants. In India, she had never said 'Please' or 'Thank you', and once she had slapped her nurse. Somehow she knew that she must not treat Martha this way.

At first Mary had no interest in Martha's chatter, but soon she began to listen to the friendly Yorkshire voice.

'Eh! You should see all my brothers and sisters in our little cottage on the moor,' Martha said. 'There's twelve of us, and my father only gets sixteen shillings a week. My mother has a job to feed 'em all for that. The fresh air on th' moor makes 'em strong and healthy. Our Dickon, he's twelve, he's always out on th' moor. He's good wi' animals.'

When Martha left, Mary went outside.

'Go and look at the gardens,' Martha had said. 'There's not much growing now, but it's lovely in summer!' She had stopped for a second and then said softly, 'One of the gardens has been shut up for ten years, ever since Mrs Craven died. Mr Craven locked the door and buried the key. He hates that garden.'

The grounds of Misselthwaite Manor were huge. They were divided by high walls, so there were many gardens. Doors led from one garden to the next, and every garden looked bare and wintry.

Presently an old man came through one of the doors. He had a surly old face and did not seem at all pleased to see Mary.

'Can I go through that door?' asked Mary.

'If tha likes,' he replied. 'There's nowt to see.'

Mary was hoping to find the door to the locked garden. She tried many doors, but they all opened easily. There was one wall covered with ivy that seemed to have no door at all. She could see trees behind the wall. A robin on a high branch burst into song. She stopped to listen, and the cheerful notes brought a little smile to her unhappy face.

Mary wandered back to the old man, who ignored her and went on digging.

At last she said, 'There's a garden over there without a door.'

'What garden?' he asked gruffly.

'On the other side of that wall,' she replied. 'I heard a robin in the trees there.'

The old man stood up and a smile spread across his face. He whistled very softly, and the robin landed by his foot.

'Here he is,' he said quietly. 'He always comes when I whistle. Isn't he a grand little chap?' The robin, plump and scarlet-breasted, hopped about, pecking at the earth. Ben Weatherstaff, the gardener, went on digging. 'He's my only friend,' he said. 'When he's not here, I'm lonely.'

'I'm lonely, too,' said Mary. 'I've never had any friends.'

Ben stopped and looked at her. 'I reckon we're a good bit alike,' he said. 'We're not good-looking and we're as sour as we look.'

Mary had never thought before about her sour face or bad temper. Now that she did, it made her feel uncomfortable. Just then, the robin flew up into a tree and sang with all his voice.

'He's taken a fancy to thee,' said Ben. 'He wants to be your friend.'

Mary looked up at the robin. 'Would you be my friend?' she asked. She spoke softly and kindly, instead of in her usual hard little voice.

'Why,' said Ben gently, 'tha said that like a real child instead of a sharp old woman. It was nearly like Dickon when he talks to th' wild things on th' moor.'

The robin flew over the wall.

'There *must* be a door to that garden,' Mary said with determination.

'Well, there's none there now,' snapped Ben. 'Don't go poking your nose in places where you don't belong.' And he walked off without saying goodbye.

ROBIN SHOWS THE WAY

Mary spent most days out of doors. The cold wind brought a pink glow to her cheeks, and each evening she ate a good meal. After supper, she liked to sit by the fire and talk to Martha.

'Why does Mr Craven hate the locked garden?' Mary asked one evening.

'It was Mrs Craven's garden. She loved it,' Martha said. 'She was sitting on the branch of a tree when it broke and she fell. She was hurt so bad, she died. That's why he hates it. He won't let anyone talk about it.'

Mary had never felt sorry for anyone before, but now she understood how very unhappy Mr Craven must be.

The wind blew across the moor and moaned and roared around the house. Martha called it 'wutherin''. Mary listened, and through the wutherin' she thought she heard a child crying.

'No,' Martha said when Mary asked. 'It's only th' wind.' And she quickly left the room.

Next day the rain poured down. 'On a day like this at home,' said Martha, 'we all keep busy indoors. Except Dickon. He goes out in all weathers. He brought home a fox cub that he found half drowned. He's got a crow, too, called Soot.'

Mary decided to explore the house. She went down corridors and up and down stairs. In the stillness, she heard again the faint sound of a child crying. As she stopped to listen, a door opened and out came Mrs Medlock. 'What are you doing here?' she demanded. 'Get back to your room at once!'

Mary was angry. She knew that she had heard the cry, and she meant to find out what it was.

The storms passed. 'Wait until th' sun shines on th' golden gorse and th' purple heather,' said Martha.

'I'd like to see your cottage on the moor, and meet your mother,' said Mary.

'Tha would love my mother,' Martha said. 'She's kind and loving and hard-working. When it's my day out and I can go home to see her, I just jump for joy.'

'I'd like to see Dickon, too,' said Mary.

'Yes, you'd like him,' Martha said. 'Everyone likes Dickon.'

'No one likes me,' said Mary sadly.

'Well, maybe that's because you don't like other people,' said Martha, smiling.

'I never thought of that,' said Mary.

Mary found Ben in the garden. 'Spring's coming,' he said. 'Th' plants are workin' under th' soil. You'll soon see crocuses and daffydowndillys.'

The robin flew over, and Mary followed him. He hopped down onto the soil and, as Mary came nearer, he pecked at the earth for a worm. Suddenly, in the soil, Mary saw a rusty key.

'Perhaps it's the key to the Secret Garden!' she thought, slipping it into her pocket.

After supper, Martha told Mary about her day at home. 'Mother has sent you a present to cheer you up.' She brought out a skipping rope and showed Mary how to skip.

'Your mother is very kind,' said Mary, wondering how Martha's mother could have spared the money to buy her a rope. Now, wherever she went, Mary skipped, and

the more she skipped, the stronger she grew.

DICKON

One morning, Mary was watching the robin on his perch on the wall, when suddenly something happened that felt like magic! A gust of wind blew the ivy on the wall, and under the leaves Mary saw a door! She felt for the key in her pocket and tried it in the lock. It was very stiff, but she could just turn it. The next second, she was in the Secret Garden!

Mary's heart thumped as she looked round. It was overgrown and untidy, but she thought it was the loveliest place. She saw green shoots of bulbs pushing up through the soil, and she pulled the weeds away to make room for the crocuses and snowdrops. Time slipped by as she went on weeding and clearing dead leaves and grass.

At supper time, she longed to share her secret with Martha, but she dared not in case she should be forbidden to go again to her

Suddenly… Mary saw a rusty key

Secret Garden. Instead, she said, 'I wish I had a bit of a garden to grow things in.'

'That's a lovely idea,' said Martha. 'I'll get Dickon to bring some garden tools and seeds to plant.'

Mary worked in her Secret Garden every day. She was careful that Ben Weatherstaff never saw where she went. One day Ben said to her, 'This fresh air is doin' thee good. Tha's fatter and not so yeller. Tha looked like a young plucked crow when tha first came.' Mary laughed. She even liked Ben on his grumpy days.

One day Mary saw a boy sitting under a tree. Two rabbits and a pheasant were near him, and a squirrel clung to the tree above him. They all seemed to be listening to the tune he was playing on a pipe.

The boy got up slowly, so as not to frighten the animals. His blue eyes smiled from his round, rosy face. 'I'm Dickon,' he said to Mary. 'I've brought tha garden tools and some flower seeds.'

His smile was so gentle and kind that Mary forgot to be shy. She felt that if animals trusted him, she could trust him, too. After a while she asked, 'Do you know about the Secret Garden?'

'I've heard of it,' he said, 'but I don't know where it is.'

'Can you keep a secret?' Mary asked. Making sure no one was watching, she led him through the door in the wall. Dickon was amazed. He looked round at all the plants and trees. 'All these will grow,' he said. 'There'll be flowers and roses everywhere in a few weeks.'

They worked together, weeding and pruning. Mary felt she had never known anyone like Dickon. Trying to speak in a warm, Yorkshire voice like Dickon's and Martha's, she asked, 'Does tha like me?'

'Eh!' he laughed. 'That I does, an' so does the robin.'

After dinner, Mrs Medlock came to take Mary to see Mr Craven. 'He's going away tomorrow, and he wants to see you first,' she said.

Mary felt awkward, and a little afraid. But Mr Craven wasn't a bit frightening, nor did he seem strange at all. His face was handsome, but looked full of worry and misery. He asked if there was anything she would like. Mary asked for a piece of garden to grow her own flowers.

'Of course,' said her uncle. 'Take

any bit that's not being used.' Mary knew which bit this would be. She could call the Secret Garden her own!

COLIN

In the night, Mary was awakened by heavy rain and the wutherin' of the wind. She couldn't sleep, and as she lay tossing in bed, she heard the crying again. 'That's never the wind,' she whispered. 'I don't care what Mrs Medlock says, I'm going to find out what that noise is.'

Candlestick in hand, she walked softly along the corridors. She saw a light shining under a door. She pushed the door open and there, lying on a four-poster bed, she saw a boy crying pitifully.

He turned suddenly and stopped crying. 'Are you a ghost?' he asked, frightened.

'No, I'm Mary Lennox,' she answered. 'Who are you?'

'I'm Mr Craven's son, Colin,' said the boy.

'So I must be your cousin,' said Mary. 'Did no one tell you I'd come to live here?'

'No. No one would dare,' replied Colin. 'I should have been afraid you'd see me. My father won't let people see me. He's afraid I'll grow up to be a hunchback. I'm always ill, so I stay here in bed. My father hates me because my mother died when I was born.'

'Have you always been here?' asked Mary.

'Nearly always,' replied Colin. 'If I go out, people stare at me. I can't stand it.'

'If you don't like people to see you,' Mary said, 'shall I go away?'

'Oh, no!' Colin answered quickly. 'Stay and talk to me.'

Mary sat on a stool next to the bed, and they talked for a long time. Colin wanted to know all about Mary. He told her how miserable and lonely he felt, even though he was given whatever he asked for.

'All the servants have to please me,' Colin said. 'It makes me ill to be angry, so everyone has to do as I say.'

'Do you think you will get well?' Mary asked.

'I don't suppose I shall,' Colin replied. 'I think I am going to die. But let's talk about something else. How old are you?'

'I'm ten, same as you,' Mary said.

'How do you know I'm ten?' he asked.

'Because the garden was locked ten years ago, when you were born,' Mary answered.

'What garden?' Colin asked, surprised.

'Just a garden Mr Craven hates,' Mary replied. 'He locked the door and buried the key.'

'What's the garden like?' Colin asked.

'No one has been allowed to see it for ten years,' Mary answered. She was careful not to let him know that she had already found it.

Colin wanted to know all he could about the garden, and they talked about the exciting things they might find there.

'I shall make them open the door,' Colin said.

'Oh, no!' cried Mary. 'Let's keep it a secret. If they open the door, it will never be a secret again. Perhaps one day we may find the door. We could go inside, and no one would know about it but us.'

'I should like that,' said Colin. 'I never had a secret before.' Tired from talking, he fell asleep, and Mary crept away.

RAINY DAYS

The next morning, Mary told Martha about the crying and how she had found Colin. Poor Martha thought she might lose her job for allowing Mary to find the young master of the house.

'You needn't worry,' Mary told her. 'Colin was pleased, and he wants to see me every day.'

'Tha must have bewitched him!' Martha cried.

'What's wrong with him?' Mary asked.

Martha told her that since he was born, Colin had not been allowed to walk. His father thought his back was weak. A famous doctor had been to see him, and had said he would get strong if less fuss was made of him. But still he was spoiled and given his own way.

'Colin thinks he will die,' said Mary. 'Do you think so?'

'Mother says there's no reason for a child to live if he can't get out in the fresh air,' Martha replied.

'It's done me good to be outside,' said Mary. 'Do you think it would help Colin?'

'Eh! I don't know,' Martha said. 'The young master had a bad tantrum when he was last taken into the garden, because he thought one of the gardeners was looking at him. He cried so much he was ill all night.'

'If he ever gets angry with me,' said Mary, 'I shan't go to see him again.'

On her next visit to Colin, Mary told him about Dickon. 'He can charm the animals on the moor,' she said. 'When he plays his pipe, they come to listen.'

'The moor sounds a wonderful place,' said Colin, 'but I'll never see it. I'm going to die.'

'How do you know?' Mary asked, feeling a little cross. Colin talked about dying almost as though it pleased him.

'Everyone says I will,' Colin replied. 'I think my father will be glad when I'm not here any more.'

'I don't believe that,' said Mary. 'That famous doctor was right. They should make less fuss of you, and they should let you go out. If you could only see Dickon, you'd want to get well!' And she told him about Dickon's family, who were so well and happy even though they were so poor.

It rained for a week, so Mary could not visit the garden. Instead, she spent her days with Colin. They read and talked and, for the first time, Colin started to laugh. He often spoke of the garden and what might be in it. Mary longed to share her secret with him, but felt that she could not yet trust him.

THE SECRET IS TOLD

Mary awoke early one morning to find the sun streaming through the blinds. When she ran down to the Secret Garden, she found that Dickon was already there.

'I couldn't stay in bed on a morning like this,' he cried. 'Look at th' garden!' The rain and the warmth had made all the new shoots push up through the earth. There were clumps of orange and purple crocuses. Mary was breathless with happiness.

A whole week had passed since Mary had last seen Dickon. She told him about finding Colin.

'If we could get him out here,' said Dickon, 'he'd forget about lumps growing on his back. We'd

be just two lads and a little lass lookin' on at th' springtime. It'd do him more good than doctor's stuff.'

When Mary went in at the end of the day, Martha told her that Colin was angry because she had not been to see him.

'I won't let that boy come if you stay with him instead of me!' Colin raged when Mary went to see him. 'You're selfish for not coming!'

'What are *you*?' snapped Mary. 'You're the most selfish person I know!'

'Well, I'm going to die!' wailed Colin.

'I don't believe it,' said Mary sourly. 'You only want people to be sorry for you. But they're not! You're too nasty!' She marched to the door and called back, 'I was going to tell you about Dickon and his fox and crow, but I shan't now.' And she shut the door firmly behind her.

Later, as she thought of Colin's lonely day, her anger faded and she felt sorry for him. 'If he wants to see me tomorrow,' she thought, 'I'll go and sit with him.'

In the night, Mary was awakened by noises in the corridor, and she could hear sobbing and screaming. 'It's Colin having a tantrum,' she thought. She

Mary was breathless with happiness

covered her ears, but she couldn't shut out the dreadful sounds.

She jumped out of bed and stamped her foot angrily. 'Somebody must stop him being so selfish!' she cried. 'He's upsetting everyone in the house!' She ran into Colin's room and shouted, 'Stop! I hate you! You'll scream yourself to death in a minute, and I wish you would!'

Colin's face was swollen and he was gasping and choking, but Mary was too angry to care. 'If you scream again, I shall scream louder!' she stormed.

'I can't stop,' sobbed Colin. 'I've felt a lump coming on my back!'

'Turn over and let me look,' Mary ordered. She looked carefully at the poor, thin back. 'There's not a lump as big as a pin,' she announced. 'Don't you ever talk about it again!'

Colin's sobbing slowly died, and Mary sat by his bed quietly comforting him until he fell asleep.

In the morning Mary found Dickon in the garden with his squirrels, and she told him of Colin's sobbing in the night.

'Eh! We mun get him out here, poor lad,' said Dickon.

'Aye, that we mun,' said Mary, using the same Yorkshire words.

Dickon laughed. 'Tha mun talk a bit o' Yorkshire to Colin,' he said. 'It'll make him laugh, and Mother says laughing's good for ill folk.'

When Mary went to see Colin, she told him about Dickon and his squirrels, Nut and Shell. They laughed and talked for a long time. Then Colin said, 'I'm sorry that I said I'd send Dickon away. I didn't mean it. He sounds like a wonderful boy.'

'I'm glad you said that,' said Mary, 'because he's coming to see you, and he's bringing his animals.'

Colin cheered up. He looked so happy that Mary suddenly decided to take a chance.

'That's not all,' she said. 'There's something better. I've found the door to the garden!'

Colin was overjoyed. 'Then shall we go in and find out what's inside?' he asked.

Mary paused – and then boldly told the truth. 'I've already been in it. That's why I could tell you so much about it. I didn't dare tell you my secret until I was sure I could trust you.'

'I SHALL LIVE FOR EVER AND EVER!'

At breakfast, Colin announced to his nurse, 'A boy and some animals are coming to see me. Bring them straight up when they arrive.'

It wasn't long before Mary heard a bleating. 'That's Dickon's lamb!' she cried. 'They're coming!'

Dickon came in smiling. He carried a lamb, and his little fox trotted beside him. Nut the squirrel sat on one shoulder and Soot the crow on the other. His other squirrel, Shell, peeped out of a pocket.

Colin stared in wonder. Dickon gently put the lamb in Colin's lap and gave him a bottle to feed it. They were all so busy and happy together.

'I'm going to see it all!' cried Colin.

'Aye, that tha mun,' said Mary, 'an' tha munnot lose no time about it.'

Colin was put in his chair, and Dickon pushed it along the paths. As they went, Mary told Colin about the places they passed. 'Here's where I met Ben,' she said, 'and this is where I saw the robin. And this,' she whispered, 'this is the garden!'

Mary opened the door, and Dickon pushed the chair inside quickly. Colin looked round for a long time, seeing all the things Mary had described. Then he cried out, 'I shall get well! I shall live for ever and ever!' That afternoon, the whole world changed for Colin.

'It's been a grand day,' said Dickon.

'Aye, that it has,' said Mary.

'Does tha think,' said Colin, 'that it was made like this 'ere all for me?'

'That's a good bit of Yorkshire!' said Mary. And they all joined in the laughter.

'I don't want this day to go,' said Colin, 'but I shall come back every day.'

'That tha will,' said Dickon, 'an' we shall soon have thee digging and walking.'

Suddenly Ben Weatherstaff's face glared down at them from the top of the wall. 'What are you doing in there?' he shouted at Mary. Then he saw Colin, and his mouth opened in surprise.

'Do you know who I am?' Colin asked.

'Aye, that I do,' Ben answered. 'Th' art th' poor cripple lad.'

Colin sat up angrily. 'I'm not a cripple!' he cried. He struggled out of the chair and, with Dickon's help, stood straight and tall. 'Look at me now!' he shouted.

'God bless thee, lad!' said Ben, and tears ran down his face.

Colin remained standing. He suddenly felt his fear leave him. 'I'm not afraid any more!' he cried. 'It's the Magic of the Secret Garden! It's working to make all the plants grow, and it will work for me.'

That evening Colin was quiet. After a long time, he said to Mary, 'I'm not going to be a poor thing any more. If I believe I shall get strong and well, the Magic will make it happen.'

MAGIC

Next day in the garden, Colin called to Mary, Dickon and Ben. 'I'm going to show you that the Magic works,' he said.

Slowly, taking a few steps at a time, Colin walked right round the garden. His face was flushed with joy.

'This must be the biggest secret of all,' he said. 'When I can walk and run well, I shall walk into my father's study and say, "Here I am, well and strong!"'

It was very hard to keep the secret. The Magic of the Secret Garden was making Colin bright-eyed and rosy-cheeked. Each day, Colin and Mary did exercises to make them strong, and they both grew plumper and healthier. Mary became pretty, and Colin no longer looked like an invalid. Everyone was amazed at the change.

Now, while the Secret Garden was working its Magic, Mr Craven was travelling in faraway places. For ten years he had been trying to run away from his sorrow and had refused to be comforted.

Then one day, whilst walking

in Austria, he sat down by a stream. Gradually he felt his mind and body relax. The peace of the place filled him, and from that moment he felt healthier and happier.

One night, he dreamt of his wife's garden at Misselthwaite Manor. The dream was so clear that he decided to return home at once. As soon as he arrived home, he went to the garden.

He walked slowly, as all his sad memories came rushing back. As he stood by the door of the Secret Garden, wondering how to find the key, he heard childish laughter from the other side of the wall.

Suddenly the door burst open and a tall, handsome boy ran out. Mr Craven gazed at him, unable to speak.

Colin stood still and recovered his breath. Then he said, 'Father, I'm Colin. You can't believe it, but it's true.'

He led his father into the garden and told him how the Magic had made everything grow, and had made him strong and well.

Mr Craven had never heard such a wonderful story. He sat by Mary and Dickon and the animals and laughed as

he had not done for years. He was so proud of his handsome, healthy son!

'Now,' said Colin, 'it needn't be a secret any more. I shall never need my chair again. I shall walk with you, Father!'

They stood up and walked towards the house. At Mr Craven's side, strong and straight as any lad in Yorkshire, walked his son.

BLACK BEAUTY

by Anna Sewell
illustrated by David Barnett

MY EARLY HOME

The very first place that I can recall was a large pleasant meadow. There were six young colts in the meadow besides me. We had great fun galloping around, although they would sometimes bite and kick.

One day, my mother whinnied to me to come to her. She said, 'The colts here are good, but they are carthorse colts, and they have not learned manners. I hope you will grow up gentle and good and never learn bad ways. Do your work well, and never bite or kick, even in play.'

My mother was a wise old horse, and I have never forgotten her advice.

As I grew older, I grew handsome. I had one white foot and a pretty white star on my forehead. My black coat grew fine and soft.

When I was four years old, Squire Gordon came to look at me. He seemed to like me, and said, 'When he has been broken in, he will do very well.' My master said he would break me in himself so that I would not be frightened or hurt.

Breaking in means to teach a horse to wear a saddle and bridle and to carry someone safely on his back. He must also learn to pull a carriage or cart, going fast

'I hope you will grow up gentle and good…'

or slow, just as his driver wishes. He has to learn never to bite or kick, nor to jump at anything he sees.

Next came iron shoes. That was frightening, but the blacksmith did not hurt me, even when he drove nails through the shoe right into my hoof.

Now that I was ready to leave home, my mother said to me, 'I hope you will fall into good hands, but a horse never knows who may buy him, or who may drive him. Some men are kind and thoughtful, like our master. Others are cruel. Remember, do your best whatever happens, and keep up your good name.'

BIRTWICK PARK

Early in May, a man came to take me to Squire Gordon's. I was taken into a big stable with four stalls and a swinging window that opened into the yard.

In the next stall to me was a pony called Merrylegs, whom the children used to ride. He was a favourite with everyone, and he and I soon became great friends.

There was a stable boy called James Howard, and the coachman was John Manly. He lived with his wife and child in the coachman's cottage, near the stables.

The next day, I was taken to my new master, so that he could try me out. I found that Squire Gordon was a very good rider, and kind to his horse as well. When we came home, his lady was at the Hall door to greet us.

'Well, my dear,' she said, 'how do you like him?'

'He has a fine spirit,' my master replied. 'What shall we call him?'

She looked up at me. 'He really is a beauty, and he has such a sweet, good-tempered face and such a fine, intelligent eye – how about "Black Beauty"?'

'Black Beauty – why yes, that shall be his name.' And so it was.

Also in our stable was a chestnut mare called Ginger. She wanted to know all about my early life, and I told her. Then she told me about her life, and it was very different from mine. No one had ever been kind to Ginger.

After she had been broken in, she was sent to a fashionable gentleman in London. 'There

I was driven with a bearing rein,' she said, 'and I really hated it. I like to hold my head as high as any horse. But just imagine, if you had to hold your head up high for hours on end! That's what happens with a bearing rein.

'I grew more and more irritable. One day, just as they were straining my head up with that rein, I began to plunge and kick. That was the end of that place! I was sold and went back to the country. Alas, the groom at the new place was rough, so I bit him. I was sold again and came here not long before you did. It's better here, of course, but for how long?'

As it turned out, kindness was all Ginger needed. Her bad temper slowly died and she became quite gentle and happy at Birtwick Park.

A STORMY DAY

One late autumn day, my master and John had to go on a long journey. I was put into the dogcart, which I enjoyed.

We went along merrily until we came to a low wooden bridge. Instead of rising in

the middle, the bridge was straight and level. That meant that the water would be nearly up to the wooden planks.

Master had to pay at the tollgate. The man there said the river was rising fast, and he feared it would be a bad night.

We started for home late in the afternoon. By then the wind was blowing so hard that a big tree crashed to the ground beside the road. I heard the master say to John that he had never been out in such a storm.

It was very nearly dark by the time we

got back to the bridge. We could just see that the water was over the middle of it, but as that happened sometimes when the river was high, Master did not stop. We were going along at a good pace, but the moment my feet touched the first part of the bridge, I knew there was something wrong. I did not dare to go forward, so I stopped dead.

'There's something wrong, sir,' said John.

He sprang out of the dogcart and tried to lead me forward. 'Come on, Beauty, what's the matter?'

Just then the man at the tollgate on the other side ran out of the house, waving a torch about and shouting at the top of his voice. 'What's the matter?' shouted my master.

'The bridge is broken in the middle and part of it is carried away. You can't cross.'

'Thank God!' said my master.

'You Beauty!' said John, and took the bridle and gently turned me round to the right-hand road by the riverside. The next bridge was much further up the river, and we had a long way to go.

At last we came home to the Hall. As we came up, Mistress ran out, saying, 'Are you really safe, my dear? Oh! I have been so anxious. Have you had an accident?'

'No, my dear, but if your Black Beauty had not been wiser than we were, we should all have been carried down the river at the wooden bridge.'

Then John took me to the stable. Oh, what a fine supper he gave me that night – a good bran mash and some crushed beans with my oats – and such a thick bed of straw! I was glad of it, for I was tired.

THE FIRE

My master and mistress decided one day to visit some friends who lived about fifty miles away. James Howard, the stable boy, was to drive them. He was leaving us shortly to go to a better job, and needed the practice in driving. The first day we travelled thirty-two miles. There were long, heavy hills, but James drove so carefully that Ginger and I were not at all harassed.

Just as the sun was going down, we reached the town

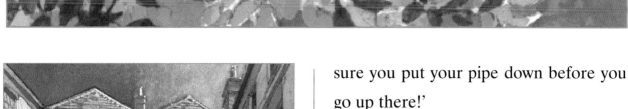

where we were to spend the night. We stopped at a big hotel in the Market Place. We drove into a long yard, and two ostlers came to take us to our stalls in a long stable.

Later on in the evening, a traveller's horse was brought in by one of the ostlers. While the ostler was grooming, a young man with a pipe in his mouth came into the stable for a gossip.

'I say, Towler,' said the ostler, 'run up into the loft and put some hay down into this horse's rack, will you? Only make

sure you put your pipe down before you go up there!'

'All right,' said the other. A few moments later I heard him step across the floor overhead and put down the hay. Then James came in for a last look at us before he went to bed. When he left, the door was locked and we were left alone.

I don't know what time of night it was, but I woke up suddenly, feeling very uncomfortable. The stable seemed full of smoke, and I could hardly breathe.

I heard Ginger coughing, and the other horses seemed restless, pulling at their halters, and many of them were stamping.

I could hear a soft rushing noise, and a low crackling. It seemed so strange that it made me tremble all over with fear.

At last Dick Towler burst in with a lantern and began to untie the horses, to lead them out. He seemed so frightened himself that he frightened us as well, and none of us would go with him.

I saw a red light flickering on the wall, and heard a roaring noise. Then there was a cry of 'Fire'.

The next thing I heard was James's voice, quiet and cheery, as it always was.

'Come on, Beauty, we'll soon be out of here.' He took the scarf off his neck and tied it lightly over my eyes, and, patting and coaxing, he led me out of the stable. When we were safe in the yard, he slipped the scarf off my eyes and shouted, 'Here, somebody! Take this horse while I go back for another.'

A man stepped forward and took me, and James ran back into the stable. I set up a shrill whinny as I saw him go. Ginger told me afterwards that whinny was the best thing I could have done for her. Had she not heard me, she would never have had the courage to come out.

There was confusion in the yard as the horses were brought out of other stables. I kept my eye on the stable door, where the smoke poured out thicker than ever, and I could see flashes of red light.

Then I gave a joyful neigh – James was coming through the smoke, leading Ginger, who was coughing violently. Suddenly there came a sound of galloping feet and loud rumbling wheels. Two horses dashed into the yard pulling a fire engine, and the firemen leapt to the ground. The flames rose in a great blaze from the roof.

Next day, everyone was wondering how the fire had started. At last an ostler remembered that Dick Towler had been smoking a pipe when he came into the stable. Dick said that he had put his pipe down, but no one believed him. Pipes were never allowed in the stable at Birtwick Park, and I thought it ought to be the rule everywhere.

JOE GREEN

After that terrible night, it was good to get home to Birtwick Park. John was equally glad to see us, and had a good deal of praise for the courage James had shown at the fire.

Before he and James left us for the night, James said, 'Who is coming in my place?'

'Little Joe Green at the Lodge,' said John. 'He is small, but he is quick, and willing and kind hearted as well.'

The next day Joe came to the stables to  learn all he could before James left. He learned to sweep the stable and bring in the new straw

28

The firemen leapt to the ground

and hay. He began to clean the harness, and helped to wash the carriage. He was too small to groom Ginger and me, so James taught him on Merrylegs. He was a nice little fellow, and always came whistling to his work.

Merrylegs was a good deal put out at being 'mauled about', as he said, 'by a boy who knew nothing.' Towards the end of the second week, however, he told me confidentially that he thought the boy would turn out well.

At last the day came when James had to leave us. He wasn't very happy about it, and he looked quite downhearted that morning. John tried to cheer him up, but everyone was sorry to lose James.

GOING FOR THE DOCTOR

Not long after James had left us, I was awakened suddenly in the night by the stable bell ringing loudly. Then John came in, saying, 'Wake up, Beauty, you must go fast now, if ever you did. The mistress is ill and we must go for the doctor.'

We went like the wind, and the church clock struck three as we drew up at Doctor White's door. John knocked at the door like thunder. Doctor White put his head out of the window. 'What do you want?' he said.

'Mrs Gordon is very ill, sir. Master wants you to go at once. He thinks she will die if you cannot get there.'

Doctor White was soon at the door. 'The worst of it is,' he said, 'my horse has been out all day and is worn out. What is to be done? Can I have your horse?'

'He has come at a gallop nearly all the way, sir, but I think my master would not be against it if you think fit, sir.'

'I will soon be ready,' said the doctor.

The way back seemed long, but I did my best.

I was glad to get home. My legs shook, and I could only stand and pant. I had not a dry hair on my body, the water ran down my legs, and I steamed all over.

For the next few days I was very ill, and Mr Bond the horse doctor came every day. John would get up two or three times in the night to come to me. My master often came to see me, too. 'My poor Beauty,' he said

one day, 'you saved your mistress's life!' I was glad to hear that – the doctor had told Squire Gordon that had we been just a little longer it would have been too late to save her.

I don't know how long I was ill, but I thought I was going to die, and I believe they all thought so, too.

When I grew well again, I found that sad changes were about to happen. We heard from time to time that our mistress was ill. Then we heard that she must go to a warm country for two or three years.

The master began immediately to make arrangements for leaving England.

We heard it talked about constantly in our stable. John went about his work silent and sad, and Joe scarcely whistled.

At last the day came when we took our master and mistress to the station. As the train glided away, John sighed. 'We shall never see her again,' he said. 'Never.' He took the reins, mounted the box and, with Joe, drove slowly home – but it would not be home to us from now on.

EARLSHALL

Next morning, Joe took Merrylegs to the vicarage, for he had been given to the vicar. Then John took Ginger and me to Earlshall Park, where we were to live.

A groom took us to a light, airy stable. In a short while, John and our new coachman, Mr York, came in to see us. John said, 'I had better mention that we have never used the bearing rein with either of these horses.'

'If they come here,' said York, 'they will have to wear the bearing rein. My lady

As the days went by, the rein grew really short. I was very unhappy, but Ginger really hated it. One dreadful day came when she kicked York's hat off and reared so much that she fell down.

After this, Ginger was used for hunting and was never put into a carriage again.

I was given a new partner called Max, but we still had to suffer the tight rein. In my old home, I always knew that John and my master were my friends. Here at Earlshall, although I was quite well treated, I had no friend. York never tried to help over that rein.

Time went on, and I grew tired and depressed, hating my work. But sadly, much worse was to come.

REUBEN SMITH'S DOWNFALL

When our master and his family went to London in the spring, they left Reuben Smith in charge of the horses that stayed behind. He was a very good man – most of the time. He had one great fault, however – the love of drink.

has to have style, and her carriage horses must be reined up tight.'

Then John came round to each of us to pat and speak to us for the last time. His voice sounded very sad. I never saw him again.

Next afternoon, we took my lady for a drive. When she came out, she said, 'York, put those horses' heads higher – they're not fit to be seen.'

York shortened the bearing rein, and I began to understand what I had heard. It made it much harder to pull uphill.

Just before the family was due to return, Smith had to go up to town, and he chose me for the journey. On the way there, he was his usual thoughtful self.

In town, however, he began to drink, and it was late when we started back. Suddenly he began to gallop, harder and harder. Sometimes he whipped me, although I was already going at full speed. I had a loose shoe, and the speed we were going at loosened it still more. It came off and I stumbled, falling on my knees. Smith was flung off by my fall and lay groaning some distance away. After a while, he stopped groaning and lay still.

At first it was thought that Reuben Smith's death was my fault. Then my sore hoof was discovered, and everyone realised that Smith must have been drinking. Later, several people said that he had been drunk when we left town.

As soon as my knees were more or less healed, I was put into a small meadow for a month or two. Ginger was there, too, and we were glad to see each other. She said that she had been ruined by hard riding and they were going to see if rest would help. We both felt we were not what we had been.

One day, the Earl came into the meadow with York. The Earl seemed very annoyed as they looked us over. 'What makes me most angry,' he said, 'is that these horses of my old friend, who thought they would find a good home with me, are ruined. The black one will have to be sold; I can't have knees like that in my stables. Try to find him a good home.'

And about a week later, I was bought by the master of some livery stables, and left Earlshall. I had become a job horse, which meant that I could be hired out to anyone who wished to drive me.

LIFE AS A JOB HORSE

Some of the people who wanted to hire me couldn't drive at all. As I was good-tempered and gentle, I was more often let out to the bad drivers than some of the others, because I could be depended upon.

Of course, we sometimes came in for good driving. One morning, I was put into a light gig and taken to a house in Pulteney Street. Two

Filcher… groomed me thoroughly

gentlemen came out. The taller of them took the reins, and I can remember even now how quietly he turned me round. Then, with a light feel of the rein and drawing the whip gently across my back, we were off.

I arched my neck and set off at my best pace because I had someone behind me who knew how a good horse ought to be driven. It seemed like old times again!

This gentleman took a great liking to me, and eventually I was sold to a friend of his, Mr Barry, who wanted a safe, pleasant horse for riding. I had yet another new master.

At first, this seemed a good change. My groom, a man called Filcher, had once been an ostler at a hotel. His wife bred chickens and rabbits for sale.

Filcher kept the stable clean and airy, and he groomed me thoroughly. He was never otherwise than gentle, and he certainly knew his job.

When I first arrived, I heard the master give the order for food – the best hay, with oats and beans, and bran with rye grass, as Filcher thought necessary. I was going to be well off!

After a while, however, I found I wasn't getting anything like the amount of oats I should have had. I grew tired and unhappy.

A farmer friend of Mr Barry's noticed this one day. He looked me over carefully, then said to my master, 'I don't know who gets the oats you pay for, but it certainly isn't your horse! I suggest you look into what's happening in your stable. Some scoundrels are mean enough to rob a dumb beast of his food.'

When Mr Barry took his advice, the police discovered that my oats were being fed to Mrs Filcher's rabbits! Filcher went to prison for two months, and in a few days' time I had a new groom.

THE HUMBUG

Alfred Smirk was a tall, good-looking fellow, but if ever there was a humbug in the shape of a groom, he was that man. He was very civil to me, and never used me ill. In fact, he did a great deal of stroking and patting when his master was there to see it.

Smirk thought himself very

handsome and spent a lot of time in front of a little mirror in the harness room. Everyone thought he was a very nice young man, but I should say he was the laziest, most conceited fellow I ever came near.

Of course, it was wonderful not to be ill used, but a horse wants more than that. I had a loose box and might have been very comfortable if Smirk had not been too lazy to clean it out and take the damp straw away. As to cleaning my feet or grooming me properly, he never did those things at all. Standing on damp straw had made my feet grow tender and unhealthy. When I stumbled twice in an afternoon, my master took me to the farrier to see what was wrong.

'Your horse has got the thrush, badly,' said the farrier. 'His feet are very tender. We find this sort of thing in dirty stables where the litter isn't cleaned out.'

He cleaned and treated each hoof in turn, and then he ordered all the litter to be taken out of my box day by day and the floor kept very clean.

My feet were soon all right again. Mr Barry, however, was so much disgusted at being twice deceived by his grooms that he decided to give up keeping a horse altogether.

I was sold again – this time into a very different kind of life. My new master was a cab driver called Jeremiah Barker, usually known as Jerry.

A LONDON CAB HORSE

That first evening, I knew I was going to be happy there. Jerry's wife, Polly, came to see me with their eight-year-old daughter, Dolly. Their son, Harry, who was twelve, had already been helping to groom me and their other horse, Captain.

Polly and her little girl made much of me, and it was a great treat to be petted again, and talked to in a gentle voice.

Polly thought I was too handsome and too good to be a cab horse, apart from my broken knees. 'We don't know whose fault that was,' said Jerry. 'I shall give him the benefit of the doubt, for I never drove a firmer, neater stepper.'

The first week of my life as a cab horse was very trying. I was anxious and harassed by the noise

and the hurry of London traffic. But Jerry was a good driver, and he took as much thought for his horses as he did for himself. He kept us very clean, and always fed us well.

But the best thing about my time there was our Sundays for rest. One lady wanted us to take her to church every Sunday, but Jerry said working seven days a week was too much for his horses as well as himself. The lady was quite cross at first, but then she saw that he was right. Jerry didn't lose her custom over it.

Christmas and the New Year are no holiday for cabmen and their horses. There are so many parties and balls that the work is hard and often late. Sometimes driver and horse have to wait for hours, shivering with cold, while the cheery people inside are dancing.

We had a great deal of late work in Christmas week. Jerry had a bad cough, and standing around in the cold made it worse. One night, when we got home, it was so bad that he couldn't speak. He gave me a rubdown as usual, although he could hardly get his breath. Then Polly brought me a warm meal, and they locked the door for the night.

The next day was very strange. Harry came in to clean and feed us, but he didn't whistle or sing as he usually did.

Two days passed like that, and there was great trouble indoors, because Jerry was dangerously ill. He grew better at last, but the doctor said that he must never go back to the cab work again.

After a while, Jerry managed to find work as a coachman. A cottage with a garden went with the job, and the family was very pleased. But I was heavy-hearted as I was led away to a sale once more.

FARMER THOROUGHGOOD AND HIS GRANDSON

As I waited at the sale, sad and full of doubt, I noticed a man who looked like a gentleman farmer. I saw his eye rest on me, and I pricked up my ears and looked at him.

'There's a horse, Willie, that has known better days,' he said to a young boy with him. He gave me a kind pat as he spoke.

'Poor old fellow! Couldn't you buy him and make him strong again, Grandpapa?' asked the boy, stroking my face. 'Just like you did with Ladybird?'

The farmer laughed. 'I can't buy every old horse and make him strong again.' As he spoke, he slowly felt my legs. 'Just trot him out, will you?' he said to the man who had brought me.

I arched my poor, thin neck, raised my tail a little and threw out my legs as well as I could, for they were very stiff.

'All right, I'll take him,' said the gentleman farmer, whose name was Mr Thoroughgood.

From then on, I had good food, perfect rest, soft turf and gentle

exercise. I began to feel quite young again!

One day in March, Mr Thoroughgood tried me out in the light carriage. My legs were no longer stiff, and I did the work with perfect ease. Mr Thoroughgood was pleased. He said to Willie, 'Now we must look for a quiet place for him, where he will be well looked after.'

One day that summer, the groom cleaned and brushed me with such care that I thought some new change must be at hand. Willie seemed half-anxious, half-merry, as he got into the carriage with his grandfather. 'If the ladies take to him,' said the old gentleman, 'they'll be suited and he'll be suited. We can but try.'

We drove through the village and up to a pretty house with a lawn and shrubbery at the front. Willie stayed with me while Mr Thoroughgood went inside. Soon he returned, followed by three ladies.

They all came and looked at me and asked questions. One lady said she was sure she should like me, I had such a good face. Another said that she would always be nervous in riding behind a horse that had once been down.

'It isn't always the horse's fault,' said Mr Thoroughgood.

'Why don't you have him on trial for a while, so that your coachman can see what he thinks?'

And so it was arranged. In the morning the ladies' smart-looking groom came to collect me. I was led home, placed in a comfortable stable, fed, and left to myself.

The next day, when the groom was cleaning my face, he said to himself, 'That is just like the star that Black Beauty had. He was much the same height, too. I wonder where he is now.'

Then he noticed my white foot and began to look me over more carefully. 'White star on the forehead, one white foot on the off-side.'

Then, looking at my back, 'And there is that little patch of white that we used to call "Beauty's threepenny bit". It *must* be Black Beauty! Why, Beauty! Beauty! Do you remember me – little Joe Green?' And he began patting and patting me as if he was quite overjoyed.

That afternoon, after I had taken the ladies for a safe, gentle drive, I heard Joe telling them that he was sure I was Squire Gordon's old Black Beauty. They were already pleased with me, so they decided to keep me and call me by my old name.

I have now lived in this happy place a whole year. Joe is the best and kindest of grooms, and my work is easy and pleasant. My ladies have promised that I shall never be sold, so I have nothing to fear; and here my story ends.

My troubles are all over, and I am at home. Often, before I am quite awake, I fancy I am still in the orchard at Birtwick, standing with my old friends under the apple trees.

THE RAILWAY CHILDREN

by Edith Nesbit
illustrated by George Buchanan

THE BEGINNING OF THINGS

They were not railway children to begin with. They lived near London, in a red brick villa that had what house advertisements call 'every modern convenience'. They only travelled by train to go to the zoo or Madame Tussaud's.

There were three of them. Roberta, whom everyone called 'Bobbie', was the eldest. Then came Peter, who wanted to be an engineer, and Phyllis, the youngest.

They had a mother who read to them, helped with their homework and wrote funny poems for their birthdays. Their father was perfect – never cross, never unfair, and always ready for fun. They were perfectly happy until, one day, a dreadful change came into their lives.

Late one evening, two men called to see their father, who was busy mending a toy railway engine for Peter. Then Father went away in a taxi.

Their mother was very upset. She asked the children just to be good and not to ask questions. Bobbie realised that something serious was making her mother miserable.

'I say,' said Phyllis, 'you used to say it

There were three of them

was so dull – nothing happening like in books. Now something *has* happened!'

'I never wanted things to happen to make Mother unhappy,' said Bobbie. 'Everything's perfectly horrid.'

Everything continued to be perfectly horrid for some weeks. Then they were told that their father, who worked for the Government, had gone away on business and might be away a long time.

Mother told them they were going away to live in a little white house in the country. All the useful household things were packed up. 'But we can't take everything,' said Mother. 'We just have to play at being poor for a bit.'

Mother and the children went down by train. When they arrived, they stood on the draughty platform and watched the rear lights of the guard's van disappear into the darkness. They did not guess then how soon the railway would become the centre of their new life.

It was a long, dark, muddy walk from the station to their new home. The rough country road led through a gate in the fields to a dark, lumpish thing Mother said was the house, Three Chimneys.

There were no lights, and the front door was locked. The carter, who brought their luggage, found the key under the doorstep, and lit a candle for them. The dark and forbidding kitchen was piled up with furniture and there was no fire in the grate. They could hear scampering and rustling in the walls.

'What's that noise?' asked the girls.

'Only the rats,' said the carter, going out. As the door shut after him, the draught blew out the candle.

'I wish we'd never come!' wailed Phyllis.

'*Only* the rats!' said Peter in the dark.

PETER'S COAL MINE

'**W**hat fun!' said Mother. 'This will be quite an adventure!'

A neighbour was supposed to have left them some supper, but they could not find any, so Mother opened one of the packing cases. There was some food in it from the store-cupboard at home, and they had a picnic meal in the kitchen.

Next morning, the children woke early and crept down to get

everything ready for breakfast before Mother woke up.

There was no water in the bedroom, so they washed under the spout of the pump in the yard. 'It's much more fun than basin washing!' said Bobbie. 'How sparkly the weeds are!'

They lit the fire, put the kettle on, and laid the table. Then they went to explore.

The house stood in a field, on a hilly slope. Down below, they could see the line of the railway, and the black yawning mouth of a tunnel. The station was out of sight. There was a bridge with tall arches running across one end of the valley.

They all sat down on a flat stone in the grass to watch for trains. Mother found them, at eight o'clock, asleep in a contented, sun-warmed bunch.

By that time, the fire had burned out and the kettle had boiled dry. But Mother had found their supper laid in another room, so they had it for breakfast – cold roast beef, bread and butter, cheese and apple pie.

All the unpacking was done by late afternoon, and Mother went to lie down. So the children decided to set off and explore the railway.

They slid down the short, smooth turf slope, set with furze bushes and yellow rocks here and there. The way ended in a steep run and a wooden fence, and there was the railway, with shining metal rails, telegraph wires, posts and signals.

Suddenly there was a rumbling sound, and a train rushed out of the tunnel with a shriek and a snort. The stones between the lines jumped and rattled.

'Oh!' said Bobbie. 'It was like a great dragon passing by!'

'I never thought we should ever get so near to a train as this!' gasped Peter.

'I wonder if that train's going to London,' said Bobbie. 'That's where Father is!'

'Let's go to the station and find out,' said Peter.

They walked along the edge of the line, pretending the sleepers were stepping stones. Once they reached the station, the children peered round a door and into the porter's room. He was half asleep, reading a newspaper.

There were a great many crossing lines at the station. Some were just sidings with trucks standing in them. In one of these there was a great heap of coal, with a line of whitewash at the top.

The porter came out and told them that the white mark was to show how much coal was there, so that he would know if any had been 'nicked'. 'So don't you go off with none in your pockets, young gentleman!' he warned Peter. (Peter was to remember this warning later.)

The children quickly settled down to their new life in the country. They got used to being without Father, though they did not forget him.

Their mother spent most of the day writing stories, and she sent them away to editors. More often than not they were returned with a kind letter, saying that the story was not suitable, but sometimes a sensible editor kept one, and then they had halfpenny buns for tea.

Mother often reminded them that they were poor now. On a cold day in June, they asked for a fire, and she said, 'Coal is so dear! Have a good romp in the attic – that will warm you up!'

This gave Peter an idea, but he would not tell the others. 'It may be wrong, so I won't drag you into it,' he said. 'But if Mother asks what I'm doing, say I'm playing at mines.'

Two nights later, he called the girls to help him, and bring the Roman Chariot. (This was an old pram they had found in a shed.) They guided it down the slope towards the station. Hidden in a hollow was a small heap of coal.

'This is from St Peter's Mine!' he said, piling it into the pram. Then they hauled the coal and the Chariot home.

Mrs Viney, their daily help, remarked how well the coal was lasting that week!

But one dreadful night the Station Master caught Peter scrabbling around in the coal heap.

'I'm not a thief!' Peter insisted. 'I'm a coal miner!' Bobbie and Phyllis, who had been hiding behind a truck, came bravely out to join Peter.

'Why, it's the children from Three Chimneys!' exclaimed the Station Master in great surprise. 'Don't you know it's wrong to steal? What made you do such a thing?'

Peter explained how his mother had said they were too poor to have a fire and that he had wanted to help. He thought it wasn't wrong to take coal from the *middle* of the pile – it was like mining, and they really did need it.

The Station Master promised to overlook it 'this once'. 'But remember, stealing *is* stealing, even if you call it mining! Now run along home to your mother!' he told them sternly. The children were thoroughly relieved that the Station Master had been so kind to them.

'You're a brick!' said Peter.

'You're a dear!' said Bobbie.

'You're a darling!' said Phyllis.

THE OLD GENTLEMAN

The children could not keep away from the railway, and the Station Master, who had forgiven them for the coal, said they could visit whenever they liked. Before long they had given the trains names. The 9.15 up was the Green Dragon. The midnight express, which sometimes woke them from their dreams, was the Fearsome Fly by Night.

As time went by they made a friend,

a fresh-faced old gentleman who travelled on the 9.15. He waved to them as they watched the Green Dragon tear out of its dark lair in the tunnel, and they waved back. They liked to think that perhaps he knew their father in London and would take their love to him.

The porter, whose name was Perks, felt sorry for the children whose father had been away for so long. He told them all sorts of fascinating things about trains, and he told them about the different kinds of engines. Peter was very keen and soon started to take a great interest in collecting engine numbers in a small notebook. He spent much of his time at the railway, always on the lookout for new numbers to add to his collection.

One day their mother was taken ill, and Peter had to fetch the doctor from the village. The doctor said that Mother was suffering from influenza, and gave her some medicine. He said she should have beef tea, brandy and all sorts of luxuries that the children knew they could not possibly afford. They were very worried.

'We've got to do something!' said Bobbie. 'Mother needs our help, otherwise she simply won't

get better!' At last they had an idea. They got a sheet and made a big notice that read:

LOOK OUT AT THE STATION

They fixed it up on the fence, and pointed at it when the train went by. Phyllis ran to the station with a letter for the old gentleman. It told how ill their mother was and what they needed, and promised to repay him when they grew up. The old gentleman read it, smiled and quietly put it in his pocket. Then he went on reading *The Times*.

That evening, Perks came to their door with a big hamper. In it was everything they had asked for, and more – peaches, two chickens, port wine, roses and a bottle of Eau-de-Cologne. There was also a letter from the old gentleman. He said it was a pleasure to help, and their mother was not to be cross with them for asking.

Two weeks later, another notice went up:
SHE IS NEARLY WELL, THANK YOU

Mother was angry at first, but she knew the children had only wanted to help.

'You must never, *never* ask strangers  for anything!' she said. 'But I must write to thank your old gentleman for his kindness.'

PRISONERS AND CAPTIVES

One day, Mother went to Maidbridge, the nearest town, to post some letters. The children went to meet her train, and as they were early, they played games in the General Waiting Room.

When the 'up' train came in, the children went to talk to the engine driver, as they often did. They were surprised to see a crowd gathered round a man with long hair and wild eyes. He was trembling and looked ill, and he was talking in a foreign language that nobody could understand. Peter asked him, 'Parlay voo Frongsay?'

The man poured out a flood of words that Peter knew were French, though he did not understand them. The children had been taught French at school. How they wished they had learned it! But their mother could speak French, and she would be on the next train.

Bobbie begged the Station Master not to frighten the man. 'His eyes look like a fox's in a trap!'

'I think I ought to send for the police,' said the Station Master.

Just then Mother's train came in. She spoke to the stranger in French, and he replied excitedly. 'It's all right,' she said. 'He's Russian, and he's lost his ticket. I'm going to take him home and I'll tell you more in the morning. He's a great man in his own country. He writes books – beautiful books – I've read some of them.'

That night Mother told the children about the Russian gentleman. He had written a book about the poor people in Russia in the time of the Tsar, and how the rich people ought to help them.

Because of this, he was put in prison and then sent to Siberia, where he was very badly treated.

'How did he get away?' the children asked.

Mother explained that prisoners were sent as soldiers to war, and he had deserted. He had come to England, to look for his wife and child, but lost his train ticket and got out at the wrong station.

'Do you think he'll find his family?'

'I hope and pray so,' said Mother. Then, after a pause, she said, 'Dears, when you say your prayers, ask God to pity *all* prisoners and captives.'

'To pity,' Bobbie repeated slowly, '*all* prisoners and captives. Is that right?'

SAVIOURS OF THE TRAIN

The Russian gentleman was soon well enough to sit out in the garden. Mother wrote to Members of Parliament and other people who she thought might know where his family could be. The children could not talk to him, but they showed their friendship by smiling and bringing him flowers.

One day, they had the idea of fetching him some of the wild cherries that grew along the cliff by the mouth of the tunnel. When they got to the top of the cutting, they looked down to where the railway lines lay.

It was like a mountain gorge, with bushes and trees overhanging the cutting. Narrow wooden steps led down to the line, with a swing gate at the top. They were almost at the gate when Bobbie suddenly said, 'Hush! Stop! What's that?'

'That' was a sort of rustling, whispering sound. It stopped then started again, louder and more like a rumbling.

'Look at that tree!' cried Peter.

A tree with grey leaves seemed to be moving, shivering and walking down the slope. Then all the trees seemed to be sliding towards the railway line.

'What is it? I don't like it!' cried Phyllis. 'Let's go home!'

'It's all coming down,' said Peter. As he spoke, the great rock on which the trees grew leaned slowly forward. The trees shivered, then rock, grass, trees and bushes

48

'It's all coming down,' said Peter

slipped right away from the face of the cutting and fell on the line with a mighty crash.

'It's right across the down line!' said Phyllis.

'The 11.29's due!' said Peter. 'We must let them know at the station, or there'll be a frightful accident!'

'No, Peter, there's not enough time,' said Bobbie. 'What can we do? We ought to wave a red flag!'

The girls were wearing red flannel petticoats. They took them off and ripped them to pieces, so that they had six flags. Peter made flagpoles from saplings and stuck them through the petticoat-rags. Then they stood, each with two flags, waiting for the train.

Bobbie was terrified. She thought that no one would notice the flags, and everyone would be killed. Then came the distant rumble and hum of the metals, and a puff of white smoke far away.

'Stand firm,' said Peter, 'and wave your flags like mad!'

'It's no good,' cried Bobbie. 'They won't see us!

The train came faster and

faster, and Bobbie ran forward as the train careered towards them.

'Keep off the line!' said Peter fiercely.

'Not yet! Not yet!' cried Bobbie, and waved her flags right over the line. The front of the engine looked enormous. Its voice was loud and harsh.

'Oh stop, stop, stop!' cried Bobbie bravely. The engine must have heard her, for it slackened speed swiftly and stopped dead. Bobbie still waved her flags, as Peter ran to meet the engine driver. Then she collapsed across the line.

'Gone off in a faint, poor little girl,' said the engine driver, 'and no wonder! She saved our lives.'

They took her back to the station in the train, and allowed her to rest. She gradually came round and began to cry.

At the station they were cheered and praised like heroes. It was all rather overwhelming.

'Let's go home,' said Bobbie, thinking what might have happened to the people.

'It was us that saved them!' said Peter.

'We never got any cherries, did we?' said Bobbie. The others thought her rather heartless.

For Valour

There were all sorts of good things about Roberta. For instance, she wanted to make other people happy. And she could keep a secret – she never said anything to let her mother know how much she wondered what she was unhappy about. That was not as easy as you might think.

Another thing about Roberta was that she tried to help people. She wanted to help the Russian gentleman find his wife and child. One day, she got her chance.

The railway decided to make a presentation of three gold watches to the children, for their brave action in saving the train. There was a little ceremony at the station, and Peter made a modest speech, saying, 'What we did wasn't anything really – at least, it was awfully exciting, and thank you all very much!'

The old gentleman was there, and Bobbie asked to speak to him in private. She told him all about the Russian – 'Mr Sczcepansky – you call it Shepansky.'

The old gentleman had heard of him, and had read his book. 'So your mother took him in,' he said. 'She must be a very good woman.'

Ten days later, the old gentleman came through the fields to see the children. 'Good news!' he said. 'I've found your Russian's wife and child!'

When Mother heard the news, her face lit up, and she spoke a few French words to the Russian. He sprang up with a cry of joy, and gratefully kissed Mother's hand. Then he sank into his chair, covered his face with his hands, and sobbed.

Bobbie crept away. She did not want to see the others just then. When she came back, the old gentleman gave the three children a big box of chocolates each.

The Russian's few belongings were packed, and they all saw him off at the station. As they walked home, Mother seemed very tired. Phyllis was talking about the Russian's baby, and how it must have grown since he saw it last. 'I wonder if Father will think *I've* grown!' she said.

Bobbie said, 'Come on, Phil, I'll race you to the gate!'

You know why Bobbie did that. But Mother only thought Bobbie was tired of walking slowly. Even mothers, who love you better than anyone else, don't always understand everything.

THE TERRIBLE SECRET

One day, Mother said to Bobbie, 'You children aren't forgetting Father, are you? You never talk about him now.'

'Yes, we do, when we're by ourselves. We thought it made you unhappy to speak about him.'

'No, Bobbie dear,' said Mother, putting her arm around her. 'Father and I have had a great sorrow – worse than you could ever think of – but it would be much worse if you were to forget him!'

'I promised not to ask questions,' Bobbie said in a small voice, 'but will the trouble last always?'

'No!' said Mother. 'The worst will be over when Father comes home, I promise.'

The next day, Peter fell over a rake in the garden and hurt his foot. He had to stay indoors, so Bobbie went down to ask Perks for any magazines people had left on the train. Perks wrapped them up in a newspaper for her to carry.

She had to wait at the level crossing for a train to pass, so she rested the parcel on the top of the gate and glanced at the printing on the paper.

Suddenly she clutched the parcel – it seemed like a horrible dream. She read on, but the bottom of the column was torn off. As soon as she got home, she ran to her room and locked the door. Then she read the column again. Her face was burning, but her hands felt icy cold. 'So now I know!' she whispered.

What she had read was headed, *'End of the Trial. Sentence.'* The man who had been tried was her father. The verdict was 'Guilty'. The sentence was 'Five years' Penal Servitude'.

'Oh Daddy!' she whispered. 'It's not true! I don't believe it! You never did it! Never, never!'

Bobbie struggled through tea, and afterwards pretended she had a headache and went upstairs. Then she went to see her mother.

She did not know what to say. At first she just cried, while her mother held her close. Then at last she pulled out the paper and pointed to her father's name.

'Oh Bobbie!' Mother cried. 'You don't believe Daddy did it, do you?

'No!' Bobbie almost shouted.

'That's right. It's not true. They've shut him up in prison, but he's done nothing wrong.'

Mother told Bobbie how the men who had come to see Father that night had arrested him for selling State secrets. Letters had been found in Father's desk that made it look true. But there was a jealous man in Father's office who wanted his job. Father thought he must have put the letters there, but he could not prove it.

'Couldn't we explain all that to somebody?'

'I've tried,' said Mother. 'Nobody will listen. All we can do is to be brave and patient, and pray.'

Bobbie wrote to the old gentleman, telling him everything, and sending the newspaper cutting. 'Think if it was *your* Daddy, how you would feel,' she wrote. 'Oh do, *do* help me. With love, I remain, your affectionate little friend, Roberta.'

THE HOUND IN THE RED JERSEY

The next day the grammar school boys were going on a paper chase. The children went up to the top of the cutting by the tunnel to watch.

In a little while the 'hare' came by. Carrying a sack of torn paper to lay a trail, he ran into the mouth of the tunnel and disappeared from sight.

Then came the 'hounds', following the trail of torn paper down the steps and into the tunnel. The last one wore a red jersey.

The children scrambled across the top of the tunnel so that they could see the 'hounds' come out at the other end. It seemed a long time before the hare came panting out of the tunnel. After him came the hounds, all very slow and tired.

'There's one more to come,' said Peter, counting. 'The one in the red jersey.'

They waited, but he did not come.

'Suppose he's had an accident! He might be lying there helpless in the path of an engine!' said Peter.

'Don't talk like a book!' said Bobbie.

They set off into the tunnel. They had to walk on stepping stones and gravel, on a path that curved downwards from the metals to the wall. Slimy trickles of water ran down the sickly green bricks. As the tunnel gradually got darker, Peter lit a candle he happened to have in his pocket.

Then they heard a humming sound along the wires by the track.

'It's a train!'

Peter pushed them into a damp, dark recess in the wall. The train roared towards them, its dragon eyes of fire growing brighter. And then, with a rush and a roar and a rattle, with a smell of smoke and a blast of hot air, the train hurtled by.

'Oh!' said the children all together, in a whisper.

'Suppose the boy with the red jersey was in the way of the train!' said Phyllis.

'We've got to go and see,' said Peter.

About a hundred and fifty yards on they saw a gleam of red. There was the red-jerseyed hound, his back against the wall, his arms limp and his eyes shut.

'Is he killed?' squeaked Phyllis.

'No, he's only fainted,' said Peter. He rubbed the boy's hands.

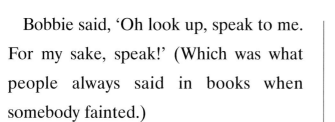

Bobbie said, 'Oh look up, speak to me. For my sake, speak!' (Which was what people always said in books when somebody fainted.)

WHAT BOBBIE BROUGHT HOME

At last the boy sighed and opened his eyes. 'I believe I've broken my leg,' he groaned. 'I tripped on these wires.'

'We're a rescue party!' said Peter proudly. 'We saw you hadn't come out of the tunnel, so we came in to look for you.'

'You've got some pluck!' the boy said, and shut his eyes again.

Peter and Phyllis set off to fetch help. Bobbie chose to stay with the 'hound' in the dark. It seemed a long time, and they held hands for comfort. Bobbie managed somehow to cut the laces on his boot and ease the swollen leg. Then men from a nearby farm came and carried the hound to Three Chimneys.

Their mother thought they had brought a *dog* home – till she saw the 'hound' was only a boy.

'Couldn't we keep him till he's better, Mother?' begged Peter.

'We'll see,' said Mother. It turned out that Jim (that was the hound's name) had no mother of his own and lived with his grandfather. His school was closing for the holidays. So Mother thought it could be arranged.

You will never guess who Jim's grandfather turned out to be.

Yes, it was the old gentleman!

When he found out what Mother had done, he knew that she could not afford

it, so he made Mother 'Matron of Three Chimneys Hospital', with a proper salary. He sent two of his own servants to help with the work.

When Jim's grandfather came, he spoke to Roberta about her letter.

'When I first read your father's case in the paper, I had my doubts,' he said. 'And since I've known who you were, I've been trying to find out things. I haven't done much yet, but I have hopes! But keep our secret a little longer. It wouldn't do to upset your mother with a false hope.'

Whether it was a false hope or not, it lit up Bobbie's face like a candle in a Japanese lantern.

THE END

Jim taught Peter to play chess and dominoes, and his leg got better and better. Life at Three Chimneys was pleasant, but also rather dull. Having servants to do everything made it seem a long time since that first morning when they had burned the bottom out of the kettle.

They hardly seemed railway children any more, because they spent most of their time at home.

'Perhaps something wonderful will happen,' said Peter one afternoon.

And something wonderful did happen, just four days later.

It was September now, and it had been a long time since the children had waved to the 9.15 and sent their love to Father by it. They decided that this morning was the perfect time to start again.

'Hurry,' said Peter, 'or we shall miss it!' They all ran, waving and shouting, 'Take our love to Father!'

The old gentleman waved from his carriage window, as he always did. Then *everybody* waved – handkerchiefs, papers and hands from every window!

'*Well!*' the children all said.

Later that morning, Bobbie decided to go for a walk down to the station. On her way, several of the villagers greeted her.

The old lady from the Post Office gave her a kiss and a hug and said, 'God bless you, dear!'

The blacksmith said, 'Good morning, Missie! I wish you joy, that I do.'

The Station Master shook her hand warmly and said, 'The 11.54's a bit late.'

Even the station cat gave Bobbie a special purr.

Finally Perks came out, holding a newspaper. 'One I must have, Miss, on a day like this!' he said.

'A day like *what*?' asked Bobbie, but before he could answer, the 11.54 steamed into the station.

Of course, *you* know what was going to happen, but Bobbie was not so clever. She felt confused and expectant, without knowing what she expected.

Only three people got out of the 11.54. A farmer's wife with a basket of live chicks. A lady with several parcels. And a third...?

'Oh, my Daddy, my Daddy!' That scream went like a knife into the hearts of everyone there.

People put their heads out to see a tall, pale man, and a little girl clinging to him while his arms went tightly around her.

As they went up the road, her father said, 'You must go in by yourself, Bobbie, and tell Mother quietly. It's all right. They've caught the man who did it. Everyone knows it wasn't your Daddy.'

'I always knew it wasn't!' said Bobbie. 'Me and Mother and our old gentleman!'

So Bobbie went in to tell Mother that the sorrow was over, and Father had come home. Father waited in the garden, looking at the flowers, the first he had seen for a long time.

Then the door opened. Bobbie called, 'Come in, Daddy! Come in!'

I think we will not follow him. It is best for us to go quietly away and take a last look at the white house where no one else is needed now.

THE WIND IN THE WILLOWS

by Kenneth Grahame
illustrated by Cliff Wright

THE RIVER BANK

The Mole had been working hard all morning, spring-cleaning his little home. There were splashes of whitewash all over his black fur, and his arms were tired.

It was spring in the world outside. Mole could feel the fresh air and sunshine calling to him in the dark, underground burrow.

Suddenly he threw his brush down.

'Bother!' he said. 'Oh, blow!' he said. 'Hang spring-cleaning!' He bolted out of the house and scrambled up the steep, narrow tunnel that was his front entrance.

He scraped and scratched and scrabbled until – *pop!* – his snout came out into the sunlight, and he found himself rolling in the warm grass of a great meadow.

'This is fine! This is better than whitewashing!' he said as he bounded joyfully across the meadow.

Suddenly he came to the bank of a River. He had never seen a River before. The water was full of life and movement, and Mole trotted beside it, fascinated.

At last he sat down to listen to the sound of the water. As he looked at the opposite bank, he saw a dark hole. Something bright and small twinkled in it. It winked, and he saw it was an eye! Then a small face appeared.

'Hang spring-cleaning!'

A brown little face with whiskers.

Small neat ears and thick silky hair.

It was the Water Rat!

The animals looked at each other.

'Hello, Mole!' said the Water Rat.

'Hello, Rat!' said the Mole.

'Would you like to come over?'

'How can I get to you?' said Mole, not knowing the ways of the River.

The Rat hauled up a little blue and white boat, just the size for two animals. He rowed across, and gave Mole his paw, to step down timidly into it.

The two animals made friends at once. Ratty was very surprised to hear that Mole had never been in a boat before.

'There is *nothing* half so much worth doing,' he told Mole, 'as simply messing about in boats.'

Then he had an idea. 'If you've really nothing else to do this morning, why don't we go down the River together and make a long day of it?'

'Let's start at once!' said Mole, settling back happily into the soft cushions.

The Rat fetched a wicker picnic basket. 'Shove that under your feet!'

'What's inside?' asked Mole.

'There's cold chicken,' said Rat, 'cold

tonguecoldhamcoldbeefpickledonions saladfrenchbreadcresssandwidgespotted meatgingerbeerlemonade –'

'Oh stop!' cried Mole in ecstasy. 'This is *too* much!'

'Do you think so?' said Rat seriously. 'It's only what I always take on these little outings.'

Rat rowed silently down the River, while Mole took in all the new sights, smells and sounds.

The Water Rat explained why he loved the River so: 'It's my world and I don't want any other.'

'But isn't it dull at times?' asked Mole. 'Just you and the River, and nobody else?'

'Nobody else! You must be joking! It's full of people – otters, moorhens, ducks and so on, about all day long!'

'What lies over *there*?' asked Mole, waving a paw towards a dark background of woodland, beyond the fields.

'Oh, that's just the Wild Wood. We don't go there much, we Riverbankers.'

'Aren't they – very *nice* people in there?' asked Mole nervously.

'Well – the squirrels are all right. The rabbits are a mixed lot. And Badger's all right. But there are others – weasels, and stoats, and foxes and so on. All right in a way. But you can't trust them.'

'And beyond the Wild Wood?'

'Beyond the Wild Wood comes the Wide World,' said the Rat, 'and that's something that doesn't matter to you or me.'

So Rat and Mole began their picnic. While they were eating, they met two of Rat's friends. One was the Otter, swimming underwater to catch fish. He climbed out on the bank, shook himself, and had a word with them. The other was Mr Badger, whose stripy head suddenly

pushed through the hedge. He grunted, 'Hm! Company!' and disappeared.

Mr Toad was on the River too – he shot past in a brand new racing skiff. He was short and fat, splashing badly, and rolling from side to side.

'He'll never do well in a boat,' said Rat.

'Not steady enough,' said Otter.

'Toad's always trying something new,' explained Rat. 'Last year he had a houseboat. But he soon gets tired of things.'

Rat and Mole went back to Rat's snug home in the River Bank and sat in armchairs beside a bright fire, chatting. Rat invited Mole to stay with him for the rest of the summer. The happy Mole went to sleep in a comfy bedroom. His friend, the River, was lapping against the bank below his windowsill, and he could hear the wind, whispering in the willows.

THE OPEN ROAD

Next day the Water Rat took Mole to visit Mr Toad, who lived nearby in a handsome house called Toad Hall.

Toad was rather rich, but not a very sensible animal. Ratty and Badger had to keep an eye on him. He was good-natured, but inclined to show off, and he was always getting into trouble.

The friends found him sitting in a deck-chair in the garden, looking at a road map. He had bought a Gipsy caravan, with an old grey horse to draw it. Toad was planning to take his first trip that afternoon, and he persuaded Mole and Rat to go along with him.

The three of them set out, but before they had gone very far, disaster struck!

They were walking along the country lane quite happily, leading the horse. Suddenly a loud *Poop! Poop!* was heard.

A magnificent motor car, all plate glass and chromium, flashed past them, flinging out a cloud of blinding dust. Then it was gone, a speck in the distance.

The poor horse was frightened and bolted. The caravan turned over and fell into the ditch.

Ratty and Mole were furious. 'You road hog!' they shouted, shaking their fists. But Toad just sat there in the dust, a dazed look in his eyes,  muttering, '*Poop! Poop!*' He did not care about the wrecked caravan. He was already thinking how marvellous it would be to drive a car.

Next day, on the River Bank, everyone was talking about the latest news.

'Have you heard? Toad went up to London early this morning. And he has ordered – what do you think? – a large and very expensive *motor car*!'

THE WILD WOOD

The long, hot summer had ended at last. Now it was winter. Mole was still staying with Ratty, on the River Bank.

One cold afternoon, the Mole decided to go to visit Mr Badger in the Wild Wood. In the winter, most animals stay at home and rest, after an active summer. Some of them go to sleep for most of the time, and you cannot persuade them to do very much. So Mole knew that if he wanted to see Mr Badger, he would have to call on him. He slipped out of Ratty's warm parlour into the open air. The

Then the pattering began. Tiny feet pursuing him, rustling through the fallen leaves. He ran, bumping into trees.

Meanwhile, Rat had discovered Mole was not at home. He saw his footprints outside, leading to the Wild Wood. Seizing a stout stick, he set out to track him. At last he found the Mole in the shelter of an old beech tree, trembling all over and so glad his friend had come.

And then it began to snow, thick and fast. Soon a white carpet covered the ground and all the paths and landmarks were lost.

Rat and Mole made their way with difficulty through the Wild Wood. Then Mole fell against something hard that cut his leg. It was a door-scraper.

'Where there's a door-scraper, there must be a door!' said Ratty sensibly. Digging down, they found a doormat, and then a very solid front door, with a brass plate with 'MR BADGER' on it, and an old-fashioned bell pull. They tugged at it.

Badger took some time to come to the door, wearing his old slippers and a thick dressing gown. He was rather grumpy at first at being disturbed, but he welcomed them into his firelit kitchen.

sky was steely. The countryside was bare. Twigs crackled under Mole's feet. Trees took on ugly, crouching shapes. The light faded. Mole began to feel frightened.

Then the faces began to emerge – little, evil, wedge-shaped faces, looking out of holes and then vanishing. Mole looked round, and saw every hole with a face in it, all fixing him with evil, sharp looks.

Then the whistling began. Very faint and shrill, behind and then ahead of him. Mole was alone, and far from help, and night was closing in.

Badger gave them a good supper, and they sat talking by the fire about Toad and his craze for motor cars. 'Something will have to be done about that,' said Badger, 'when the winter is over.'

In the morning, they had porridge for breakfast, with two young hedgehogs who had got lost on their way to school. Badger showed them all the back door out of his lair, through a maze of tunnels that led to the edge of the wood.

Mole and Rat looked back at the Wild Wood, black, threatening and grim against the snow, and made their way quickly home, safe once more on the friendly River Bank.

HOME, SWEET HOME

It was almost Christmas. Mole and Rat had been out exploring the countryside. It was getting dark when they passed through a country village. Firelight and lamplight shone in the windows. They could see children being put to bed, a man knocking out his pipe on a

smouldering log and, in one window, the shadow of a bird cage, with a sleepy bird ruffled up in its feathers. They felt tired, cold and lonely, and far from home.

The two animals plodded on across the field. Mole had his nose to the ground. As he sniffed, he felt a tingle, like an electric shock. Animals can pick up signals from smells that humans never notice. This particular smell meant *home* to Mole.

In the excitement of his new life, Mole had forgotten his own little home. But now it all came back to him, and he called to Ratty to stop.

But Ratty did not hear, and cried, 'Oh, come on, Mole! Don't hang behind!'

Poor Mole stood alone in the road. He wanted so badly to follow the scent, but he could not desert his friend. He struggled on, slowly.

Soon Ratty noticed how quiet his friend was, and how he was dragging his feet. Then he heard a sniff and a stifled sob, and it all came out.

'I know it's only a shabby little place,' sobbed Mole, 'but it was my own, and I was fond of it.'

'What a selfish pig I've been,' thought Ratty. And he turned

They passed through a country village

Mole round and they set off back the way they had come, to pick up the scent.

At last, after several false starts, Mole crossed a ditch, scrambled through a hedge and dived down a tunnel. At the end of it was a little door with 'MOLE END' painted on it. Mole lit a lantern and they could see a neat forecourt, with a garden seat, some hanging baskets with ferns, and a plaster bust of Queen Victoria.

Inside, everything was dusty and rather shabby. Mole began to feel ashamed at having brought his friend there. But Ratty ran to and fro, exploring rooms and cupboards. He started to light a fire, while Mole got busy with a duster.

'What a capital little house this is!' Rat called out cheerfully. 'So compact and well planned!'

'But I haven't got anything for supper!' Mole wailed.

'Rubbish!' said the Rat. 'I spy a sardine tin opener, so there must be some sardines.' They found some biscuits and were just about to open the sardines, when there was a scuffling noise in the forecourt, a lot of coughing, and a murmur of tiny voices.

'What's that?' asked Rat.

'It must be the field mice,' answered Mole. 'They go round at this time of year, carol-singing.'

They opened the door, and there, in the light of a lantern, eight or ten little field mice stood in a semicircle.

They wore red knitted scarves round their necks, and they jigged up and down to keep their feet warm.

'One, two, three!' cried the eldest one, and their tiny voices rose in a carol about the animals in the stable at Bethlehem.

Who were the first to cry Nowell?
Animals all, as it befell,
In the stable where they did dwell!
Joy shall be theirs in the morning!'

Mole and Rat welcomed the little carol-singers in, and Ratty sent one of them off with a basket and some money to buy food. The rest of the mice sat by the fire, drinking hot punch. When the messenger returned, they had a splendid supper.

They finally clattered off home, with presents for their families. Mole and Rat tucked themselves into bed in handy sleeping bunks. Before he closed his eyes, Mole looked happily about his old room in the glow of the firelight.

Thanks to his friend's kindness, Mole's pleasure in his old home had returned. 'Everyone needs a place of his own to come back to,' he thought drowsily, before he dropped off to sleep.

MR TOAD

One morning in early summer, Badger kept his promise to visit Ratty and Mole.

'It's time we did something about Toad,' he grunted. 'He's a disgrace to the neighbourhood. What his father would have said about his doings, I don't like to think. This craze for motor cars is getting him into trouble with the police!'

'Yes, he's had several crashes,' agreed Rat. 'I hear he has ordered another new car this week.'

They set off for Toad Hall. Sure enough, there at the front door stood a shiny, brand new, bright red motor car. Mr Toad, in goggles, cap, gaiters and a huge overcoat, came swaggering down the steps, putting on his big leather driving gloves.

'You're just in time for a jolly spin, you fellows!' he called out cheerfully.

'Oh, no, you don't!' said Badger gruffly, seizing him by the scruff of the neck and marching him back into the house. Mole and Rat took off his ridiculous motoring togs, and Badger gave him a talking-to.

Toad refused to give up driving, so they locked him in his bedroom to think it over.

But cunning Toad pretended to be ill, and while they were fetching the doctor, he skipped out of the window and bounced off to the village, laughing at his own cleverness and murmuring, 'Poop! Poop!'

At the inn he saw a beautiful motor car,

whose owners were inside having lunch. Toad could not resist trying it out. He hopped in and drove off in a cloud of dust.

Toad's next appearance was as a limp and sorry prisoner at the Magistrate's Court. He was charged with dangerous driving, stealing a motor car, and, worst of all, cheeking the police. He was sentenced to twenty years' imprisonment.

The wretched Toad was handcuffed and marched across the square to the ancient castle, guarded by men-at-arms and warders. He was dragged through courtyards where bloodhounds strained at their leashes. Down spiralling stone staircases he went, down to the deepest dungeon of all. In front of the heavy nail-studded door sat an old gaoler with a mighty bunch of keys.

The unhappy Toad realised what a foolish animal he had been. He could never hope to escape from the best-guarded prison in England.

'What has happened to the clever, popular Mr Toad, respected by everybody?' he whimpered. 'O wretched animal, so justly punished!'

He refused all food and lay limply on his bed, fat tears rolling down his cheeks.

TOAD'S ESCAPE

The gaoler's daughter was a kind young girl who was very fond of animals. She took pity on Toad, and coaxed him to eat some hot buttered toast, asking him to tell her all about Toad Hall. Soon the Toad revived a little, and began to boast about his home and his possessions.

In spite of his conceit, the young girl was sorry for him. She hated to see animals shut up. So she thought of a plan to help him to escape. He was to dress in her aunt's clothes.

Her aunt was a washerwoman, who came to the castle once a week. She was short and stout (like Toad!) Toad did not like the idea of dressing up as a poor old woman, but in the end he agreed.

The gaoler's daughter giggled as she tied the bonnet strings under Toad's chin. 'You look exactly like her!' she laughed (much to Toad's annoyance). 'Goodbye, and good luck! Be careful what you say to the sentries!'

There were some anxious moments as Toad set off, especially as the sentries made rude remarks. But Toad entered into the spirit of the thing, for he fancied himself as an actor. Soon he came through the prison gate into the sunlight. He was free at last.

He made for the railway station and was about to buy a ticket when he realised he had left his waistcoat, with all his money, in his cell. What could he do now? Then he spotted an engine driver, cleaning down his steam engine.

'Oh, sir,' cried Toad, 'I'm a poor washerwoman who's lost her purse. How am I going to get

home, and what will my little children do without me?'

The kind engine driver said, 'Tell you what, missus, I'll give you a ride on my footplate, and you can wash some shirts for me when you get home.'

Toad accepted eagerly and hopped up on the engine. They got up steam and set off. They were soon thudding away down the track, with a trail of white smoke and a whooping whistle.

Suddenly the engine driver looked back. 'There's another train following!' he cried. 'It's full of people – policemen with truncheons – plain clothes men with bowler hats – prison warders with sticks – all shouting "Stop! Stop!"'

Toad fell on his knees among the coal and begged for help. 'I am not a washerwoman at all,' he confessed. 'I am the well-known, daring criminal, Mr Toad. Please help me.'

The engine driver hated to see an animal hunted. 'Never mind, I'll help you,' he said. 'When we get through this tunnel, I'll slow down, and you can jump off and hide in the wood.'

They piled on more coal to get up speed, and the sparks flew as

Toad saw the chance of a lift

they roared through the tunnel. Then they slowed down. Toad jumped off and rolled down the bank into the wood. He laughed as he saw the other train tear past, full of policemen and warders, waving their weapons and shouting '*Stop!*'

Then he found an old tree, and lay down on a bed of leaves to wait for morning.

THE FURTHER ADVENTURES OF TOAD

Toad was getting nearer and nearer to home, and still had on his washerwoman's disguise. Presently he came to a towpath that ran alongside a canal. An old horse was plodding along it, pulling a gaily painted barge. A stout woman sat in it, her brawny arm along the tiller.

Toad saw the chance of a lift, so he told his tale of losing his purse and having to get back to his children.

'I'll give you a lift as far as Toad Hall,' the barge-woman said, 'if you'll do my dirty washing for me.' Toad had been boasting what a good washerwoman he was, so he could hardly refuse!

She gave him a great pile of washing, some soap and water in a big tub. Toad had no idea how to set about it. Soon he was puffing and blowing and rubbing and dubbing, but the clothes were no cleaner.

The barge-woman took a closer look at him. 'You're no washerwoman!' she shrieked. 'You're a dirty, ugly toad! Get off my nice clean barge!'

Toad was so annoyed that he jumped off the barge, undid the tow-rope and rode off on the horse, leaving the woman shaking her fist at him.

He galloped along, thinking how clever he was. By now he was hungry, and as he passed a hedge, the most delicious smell floated over it. A Gipsy was cooking a stew in an iron pot on a fire. Quickly Toad struck a bargain. He sold the horse for a few pence and a plate of stew.

He was feeling his old self again and began to make up a boastful song about his adventures:

'The world has held great heroes,
As history books have showed,
But never a name to go down to fame
Compared with that of Toad!'

Suddenly he heard a familiar noise. Along the highway came a motor car – the very one Toad had stolen!

Toad pretended to faint, and the car stopped. The passengers took him to be a poor washerwoman and put him in the front seat, where the fresh air would revive him.

Toad soon perked up enough to ask a favour. 'I've always wanted to see if I could drive a motor car,' he said longingly. 'Please let me try!'

The passengers were very amused to think of a humble washerwoman wanting to drive. 'Let her have a go!' they said to the chauffeur.

Toad drove off, slowly at first, then faster.

'Be careful, washerwoman!' they cried.

'I'm not a washerwoman!' said he. 'I'm the great, the famous Toad!' And he drove faster than ever, terrifying the passengers, until he took a corner too fast and drove straight into a pond.

He jumped out and hopped across the fields, leaving the passengers standing up to their waists in muddy water. But when he looked back, he saw the chauffeur and two policemen running after him.

Poor Toad puffed along. He was a very fat animal, and they were gaining on him.

Suddenly he tripped. He had come to the River Bank, and – *splash!* – he fell into the water.

He swam along, gasping, till he came to a hole in the bank. He clutched the edge and looked in.

A small, bright thing shone and moved towards him. A face grew up around it.

Brown and small, with whiskers.

Grave and round, with neat ears.

It was the Water Rat!

THE BATTLE FOR
TOAD HALL

When Toad was dry and dressed in one of Ratty's suits, Rat told him what had happened while he had been away.

The Wild Wooders had taken over Toad Hall. Weasels, ferrets and stoats were living there, eating Toad's food and drinking his drink and telling everybody that he was never coming back.

Toad was all for going up there at once and turning them out. But Ratty explained that they had armed sentries posted and all the entrances were guarded. There was no way in.

Just then Badger and Mole came in. Badger said solemnly, 'Welcome home, Toad. Alas, what am I saying? This is a poor homecoming. Unhappy Toad.' And he sat down to eat a piece of cold pie.

But Mole danced round Toad joyously and said, 'You must have escaped! O *clever* Toad!'

At this, Toad began to tell all his adventures and show off to the admiring Mole.

'Don't egg him on, Mole,' said Ratty. 'We have to think what to do next.'

They all began to talk at once, until they were silenced by the Badger. 'Be quiet, all of you,' he growled. 'Toad, you bad, troublesome little animal! Aren't you ashamed of yourself? What do you think your father, my old friend, would have said if he'd known of your goings-on?'

Toad rolled over and began to sob.

'Never mind that!' said Badger. 'We'll let bygones be bygones. I'll tell you my plan to get Toad Hall back again. There is an underground passage...' And the Badger outlined his plan.

The secret passage came up inside Toad Hall, in the butler's pantry, next to the banqueting hall. That night, there was to be a birthday party for the Chief Weasel. Everyone would be in the banqueting hall, except for a few sentries.

Badger and his men would creep along the tunnel, armed to the teeth, then come up inside the Hall and take the Wild Wooders by surprise.

Badger had a pile of weapons, and Ratty set them out in four heaps. He ran from one to the other, muttering, 'Here's a sword for the Rat, here's a sword for the Mole, here's a sword for the Toad, here's a sword for the Badger! Here's a pistol for the Rat, here's a pistol for the Mole...' and so on, till they were all sorted out.

After supper, when it was dark, they put on their belts and pistols and swords and set off. Badger led the way, flourishing a thick stick.

They kept stopping in the darkness, and bumped into one another several times. But soon they heard the noise of the feast overhead – the stamping of little feet, the clinking of glasses, and cheers.

'Now, boys, all together!' said Badger, and heaved at the trap door. They came up into the butler's pantry, and could hear the Chief Weasel giving a speech of thanks.

'I should like to say a word about our kind host, Mr Toad,' he sniggered. '*Good* Toad! *Modest* Toad! *Honest* Toad!' Everyone laughed.

'In return for his hospitality,' the Chief Weasel went on, 'I have made up a little song about him!' He began to sing a very rude song, all about motor cars and prison.

'Let me get at him!' said Toad.

'*Now!*' cried the Badger, and they burst into the hall, brandishing their weapons.

My! What a squeaking and a squealing and a screeching filled the air!

Terrified weasels dived under the tables. Ferrets rushed madly for the fireplace and got stuck in the chimney.

The mighty Badger laid about him with his stick. Mole gave a terrible war cry: 'A Mole! A Mole!' Rat flourished his pistol. Toad, swollen with injured pride, went straight for the Chief Weasel. There were only the four of them, but to the Wild Wooders they seemed like an army.

At last the room was clear, and all the

weasels fled back to the Wild Wood, except for a few Mole had given brooms and aprons, and set to tidying up the Hall.

THE WANDERER'S RETURN

Next day, Toad wanted to give a banquet to celebrate his homecoming. He spent the morning making out a programme, full of songs (by Toad) and speeches (by Toad).

When his friends saw it, they told him, 'You *must* turn over a new leaf, Toad, and stop showing off!'

Poor Toad! He had to promise to reform. But up in his bedroom, looking in the mirror, he sang his last little song in praise of himself.

'*The Toad – came – home!*

There was smashing in of window

and crashing in of door,

There was chivvying of weasels

that fainted on the floor,

When the Toad – came – home!

Shout – Hooray!

And let each one of the crowd

try and shout it very loud,

In honour of an animal

of whom you're justly proud,

For it's Toad's – great – day!'

Toad sang this very loudly, with expression, and when he came to the end, he sang it again.

Then he went quietly downstairs to greet his guests. He refused to take any credit for the victory. 'No, no, it was all Badger's idea. Mole and Rat did most of the fighting,' he said modestly. Mole and Rat looked at each other. This was indeed an altered Toad!

The gaoler's daughter and the engine driver were sent presents and letters of thanks. The barge-woman was sent the value of her horse, though Toad protested. The Gipsy was sent nothing, as he had done rather well out of the deal.

The four friends sometimes took a stroll together in the Wild Wood of a summer evening. Respectful mother weasels pointed them out to their young ones, and told them to behave or the terrible, great grey Badger would get them. This was somewhat unfair to Badger, who was fond of children. But it never failed to make them behave.

ALICE IN WONDERLAND

by Lewis Carroll
illustrated by David Frankland

DOWN THE RABBIT HOLE

Alice was tired of sitting by her sister on the grassy bank and having nothing to do. Her sister was reading a book that looked very dull.

It was a hot day, and Alice was sleepy. She was wondering whether to get up and make a daisy chain, when suddenly a white rabbit with pink eyes ran close by her.

'Oh dear! Oh dear! I shall be late!' the White Rabbit said. He took a watch out of his waistcoat pocket, looked at it and hurried on.

Alice had never seen a rabbit with a waistcoat before, nor one with a watch to take out of his pocket. She jumped up and ran after him, just in time to see him pop down a large rabbit hole under the hedge. Alice followed him, never thinking how she was going to get out again.

Suddenly Alice found herself slowly falling down a very deep well. 'I wonder how many thousands of miles I've fallen?' she thought. 'I must be somewhere near the centre of the earth. Perhaps I'll fall right through to the other side!'

But just then, *thump, thump, thump,* down she came on a heap of leaves, without hurting herself at all. Ahead of

A white rabbit… ran close by her

her, at the end of a long passage, she saw the White Rabbit hurrying along. 'Oh, my ears and whiskers, how late it's getting!' she heard him say as he turned the corner.

THE GOLD KEY

By the time Alice reached the corner, the White Rabbit had gone. She found herself in a long hall lit by lamps in the ceiling. There were doors all the way round, but they were locked. How was she going to get out?

She then saw a little table made of glass. On top of it was a gold key. But it was too small to unlock any of the doors. Then Alice noticed a low curtain. Behind it she found a tiny door, only fifteen inches high. The key fitted perfectly!

Alice had to kneel down to look through the door. There was a small passage, not much larger than a rat hole, that led to the loveliest garden she had ever seen. But she was too big to get her head through the doorway.

'I wish I could shut up like a telescope!' she said to herself.

She walked back to the glass table. To her surprise there was a bottle on it which had not been there before. A label round its neck said DRINK ME. Alice took a sip. It was delicious, so she drank it up.

'What a curious feeling!' said Alice. 'I *must* be shutting up like a telescope!' And so she was! Soon she was only ten inches high, just the right size to go through the little door into the lovely garden.

But poor Alice! When she got to the door, she realised that she had left the gold key on top of the glass table, and now she was too small to reach it. She tried to climb up one of the table legs, but it was too slippery. At last, tired out, she sat down and cried.

Then she noticed a little glass box on the floor, just under the table. Inside it was a very small cake with the words EAT ME beautifully marked on it in currants.

'Well, I'll eat it,' thought Alice. 'If it makes me larger, I can reach the key, and if it makes me smaller, I can creep under the door. So either way I'll get into the garden.'

She nibbled the cake, and soon she had finished it all up.

THE POOL OF TEARS

'Curiouser and curiouser!' cried Alice. 'Now I'm opening out like the largest telescope that ever was!'

Her feet were so far away that she wondered how she would get her shoes and stockings off and on. Then her head struck against the ceiling. Alice was more than nine feet tall!

She picked up the little gold key and hurried off to the garden door. But poor Alice could only look into the garden with one eye, by lying down on the floor. She sat down and began to cry again. 'What a great baby you are!' she scolded herself, but she could not stop crying. Soon there was a large pool of tears around her, reaching halfway down the hall.

After a while, she heard a pattering of feet in the distance. Alice dried her eyes and saw the White Rabbit coming back. He was carrying a fan and a pair of white gloves and muttering, 'Oh, the Duchess! Oh, the Duchess! Won't she be cross if I've kept her waiting!'

'Please, sir, could you help me?' asked Alice timidly. But when he saw her, the White Rabbit dropped his fan and gloves and scurried off as quickly as he could.

Alice picked up the things he had dropped. It was very hot, so she began to fan herself. She felt very strange.

'I'm not at all my usual self!' she thought. 'Perhaps I've changed into somebody else! I'll see if I still know the things I learned at school: four times five is twelve, and five times

six is thirteen... London is the capital of Paris, and Paris is the capital of Rome... That can't be right!' she sobbed. 'I *must* be somebody else!'

Then she noticed that she had managed to put on one of the White Rabbit's little gloves. 'I'm small again!' she cried, and ran off to the garden door. But now it was shut, and the gold key was back on the glass table.

'Now things are worse than ever!' she thought. Her foot slipped, and *splash!* she was up to her chin in salt water, in the pool of tears.

THE MOUSE'S TALE

Alice soon found that she was not alone: a mouse was swimming a little way off. To Alice it looked as big as a hippopotamus.

'Oh, Mouse,' she said politely, 'do you know the way out of this pool?' The Mouse did not answer.

'Perhaps it's a French mouse and doesn't speak English,' thought Alice. She only knew

one sentence in French from school. '*Où est mon chat?*' she asked hopefully.

The Mouse nearly jumped out of the water and quivered with fright.

'Oh, I beg your pardon!' apologised Alice. 'I forgot mice don't like cats!'

'Would *you* like cats – or dogs – if you were me?' squeaked the Mouse indignantly.

'I suppose not!' said Alice, and they swam together to the shore.

A strange, bedraggled collection of birds and animals had gathered there. They were running races in circles, organised by a dodo, and Alice and the Mouse watched them with great interest.

When the races were finished, Alice asked the Mouse to tell her about himself, and why he hated 'C and D'. (She was afraid to say 'cats and dogs'!)

'Mine is a long and sad tale,' he said, sighing.

Alice had been looking at the Mouse's tail as he spoke. 'It *is* long,' she said, 'but why do you call it *sad*?'

So when he began his story, Alice's idea of it was something like this:

80

'Fury said to a mouse,

that he met in the house,

"Let us both go to law: *I* will

prosecute *you*. Come,

I'll take no denial,

we must have the

trial, for really this

morning I've nothing

to do." Said the

mouse to the

cur, "Such a

trial, dear Sir,

with no jury

or judge, would

be wasting

our breath."

"I'll be judge,

I'll be jury,"

said cunning

old Fury.

"I'll try

the whole

cause

and

condemn

you

to

death." '

'You're not attending,' the Mouse said. 'Yes, I am!' said Alice. But the Mouse was offended and went away.

ADVICE FROM A CATERPILLAR

Meanwhile, the White Rabbit's fan and gloves had vanished. So had the pool of tears, the hall and the glass table. Alice found herself on the edge of a wood.

She ran till she came to a mushroom that was as big as she was. On top of it sat a caterpillar, quietly smoking a hookah, which is a sort of long, curly water pipe.

At first the Caterpillar took no notice of Alice. But after a while, it took the hookah out of its mouth and asked in a sleepy voice, 'Who are *you*?'

Poor Alice was not at all sure who she was. 'I can't remember things as I used to, and I don't stay the same size for ten minutes together,' she said.

'What size do you want to be?' asked the Caterpillar.

'I should like to be a *little* larger than I am now!' Alice replied. 'Three inches is such a silly size to be!'

The Caterpillar drew itself up to its full height, which was exactly three inches tall! 'It is a very good height indeed!' it said angrily, and began to crawl away.

As it went, the Caterpillar remarked, 'One side will make you taller, and the other side will make you shorter.'

'One side of what?' asked Alice.

'Of the mushroom, of course!' said the Caterpillar crossly. A moment later it was out of sight.

Alice put her arms round the

edges of the mushroom, as far as she could reach, and broke off two pieces. She nibbled each piece in turn till she had managed to bring her height up to just nine inches. Then she set off again till she came to a house.

Alice went up to the door and knocked timidly. There was a most extraordinary noise going on inside – howling, sneezing, and every so often a crash as if a dish had been broken. There was no answer to her knock, so Alice marched in.

PIG AND PEPPER

The door led into a large kitchen full of smoke. A duchess was sitting in the middle of the room, nursing a baby. A cook was leaning over the fire, stirring a pot full of soup and shaking pepper into it.

The air was thick with pepper. The Duchess was sneezing, and the baby was howling and sneezing in turns. A large cat was lying on the hearth rug, grinning from ear to ear.

'Why does your cat grin like that?' asked Alice.

'What size do you want to be?' asked the Caterpillar

'It's a Cheshire Cat!' said the Duchess. 'PIG!'

Alice, startled, thought the Duchess was addressing her. But it was the baby she meant.

Suddenly the cook began throwing soup over everything. Then she threw the poker and tongs, saucepans, dishes and plates at the Duchess and the baby.

'Oh, mind what you're doing!' cried Alice, as a large saucepan lid whizzed past the baby's nose.

The Duchess took no notice and began to sing a lullaby to the baby. She threw it up and down, giving it a violent shake at the end of each line.

'Speak roughly to your little boy,
And beat him when he sneezes:
He only does it to annoy,
Because he knows it teases.'

CHORUS

(with which the cook and the baby joined in)

'Wow! Wow! Wow!'

'Here!' said the Duchess, flinging the baby at Alice. 'You may nurse it for a bit. I must get ready to play croquet with the Queen.'

Alice could hardly hold the

baby, it wriggled so. She took it outside and looked at its face. It had a turned-up nose and very small eyes. Suddenly it grunted. Alice looked at it in alarm. It had turned into a *PIG*!

She put it down quickly, and it trotted happily away into the wood. 'It would have been an ugly child,' thought Alice. 'But it makes quite a handsome pig!'

Next moment, Alice was surprised to see a Cheshire Cat sitting on the branch of a tree and grinning down at her.

'Does anyone else live near here?' Alice asked.

'In *that* direction,' said the Cat, waving its right paw, 'lives a Hatter. And in *that* direction,' waving its other paw, 'lives a March Hare. Visit either: they're both mad. We're all mad here. I'm mad. You're mad.'

'Why am *I* mad?' said Alice.

'You must be,' said the Cat, 'or you wouldn't have come here. Are you going to play croquet with the Queen today?'

'I haven't been invited yet,' said Alice.

'*I'll* be there!' said the Cat, and  vanished. Suddenly it appeared again. 'What became of the baby?' it said.

'It turned into a pig,' said Alice. 'I wish you wouldn't disappear so quickly! It makes me giddy!'

'All right,' said the Cat. 'I'll do it another way.' And this time it vanished quite slowly, beginning with the end of its tail and ending with its grin, which remained hovering in midair for some time after the rest of it had gone.

'Well, I've often seen a cat without a grin,' said Alice. 'But I've never seen a grin without a cat before!'

THE MAD HATTER'S TEA PARTY

Alice easily recognised the March Hare's house. The chimneys looked like ears, and the roof was covered with fur.

At a table in front of the house, the March Hare and the Hatter were having tea. A dormouse was sitting between them. It was asleep, and the other two were using it as a cushion, resting their elbows on it and talking over its head.

The table was a large one, but all three were crowded together at one corner of it. 'No room! No room!' they cried, when they saw Alice coming.

'There's plenty of room,' said Alice, sitting down in a large armchair.

'Have some wine!' said the March Hare.

'I don't see any wine,' said Alice.

'There isn't any!' said the March Hare.

'It wasn't very polite of you to offer it, then!' said Alice angrily.

'It wasn't very polite of *you* to sit down without being asked!' said the March Hare.

Then the Hatter joined in. 'Why is a raven like a writing desk?' he asked Alice.

'I believe I can guess that…' began Alice.

'Do you mean you think you can find out the answer?' asked the March Hare.

'Exactly so,' said Alice.

'Then you should say what you mean,' said the March Hare.

'I do,' Alice replied. 'At least, I mean what I say, and that's the same thing!'

'Not the same thing at all!' said the Hatter. 'You might as well say that "*I see what I eat*" is the same thing as "*I eat what I see*"!'

'You might as well say,' added the March Hare, 'that "*I like what I get*" is the same thing as "*I get what I like*"!'

While Alice thought about how to reply to this, the Mad Hatter took out his watch and looked at it. He shook it every now and then and held it to his ear.

'Two days wrong!' he said. 'I told you butter wouldn't suit the works!' He looked angrily at the March Hare.

'It was the *best* butter!' said the March Hare.

'Yes, but some crumbs must have got in as well,' the Hatter grumbled. 'You shouldn't have put it in with a bread knife!'

The March Hare took the

watch and looked at it gloomily. 'Let's change the subject,' he said. 'I vote the young lady tells us a story.'

'But I don't know one!' said Alice in alarm.

'Then the Dormouse shall!' they both cried. 'Wake up, Dormouse!' They pinched it on both sides at once, and the Hatter poured a little hot tea on its nose.

'I wasn't asleep!' murmured the Dormouse. 'I heard every word you said!'

'Tell us a story!' said the March Hare.

'Yes, please do,' said Alice.

'Once upon a time there were three sisters,' began the Dormouse. 'Their names were Elsie, Lacie and Tillie, and they lived at the bottom of a well.'

'What did they live on? Why did they live at the bottom of a well?' Alice asked.

'Treacle. It was a treacle well,' said the Dormouse. 'These sisters were learning to draw, you see.'

'What did they draw?' asked Alice.

'Treacle,' replied the Dormouse.

'I don't understand,' said Alice. She was very confused. 'Where did they draw the treacle from?'

'You can draw water from a water well,' said the Hatter, 'so

The Hatter poured a little hot tea on its nose

why shouldn't you draw treacle from a treacle well?'

'But they were *in* the well!' cried Alice.

'Of course they were,' said the Dormouse. '*Well* in!' He was getting sleepy again. 'They drew everything that begins with an M,' he went on drowsily, 'such as Mousetraps and the Moon and Muchness. You say "Things are much of a Muchness" – did you ever see a drawing of a Muchness?'

'I don't *think* –' began Alice.

'Then you shouldn't *talk*!' snapped the Hatter.

This was too much for Alice. She got up and walked into the wood. When she looked back, she saw the others trying to put the Dormouse into the teapot.

THE QUEEN'S CROQUET GROUND

Alice noticed a tree trunk in front of her, with a door in it. She opened it and found herself back in the hall with the glass table and the gold key.

'This time I know what to do!' she said. She nibbled at the mushroom until she was small enough to go through the little door into the lovely garden.

Alice was surprised to see three gardeners busily painting a white rose tree red, and even more surprised when she saw that they were playing-cards. Their names were Two, Five and Seven.

'You see, miss, this here rose tree ought to have been red,' Two was explaining. 'If the Queen sees it, we shall all have our heads chopped off.'

'Hush!' whispered Five. 'Here she comes!' All three fell flat on their faces. There was a sound of footsteps, and Alice looked round, eager to see the Queen.

First came ten soldiers, carrying clubs. Then came ten courtiers, decorated with diamonds. Then came the ten royal children, with hearts on their tunics. Next came the guests, including the Duchess and the White Rabbit. And then came the Knave of Hearts, carrying a crown on a red velvet cushion. Last of all came the King and Queen of Hearts themselves.

Alice curtsied and told the Queen her name. 'I needn't be

afraid of them!' she thought. 'They're only a pack of cards!'

The Queen looked at the gardeners, lying flat on the ground. 'Turn them over!' she said to the Knave.

The gardeners jumped up and started bowing. 'Off with their heads!' cried the Queen, and the procession moved off.

'You shan't be beheaded!' said Alice, popping the gardeners into a flowerpot.

'Get to your places!' shouted the Queen in a voice like thunder.

It was the strangest game of croquet

Alice had ever seen. The balls were curled-up hedgehogs, and the mallets were flamingos. The soldiers doubled up and stood on their hands to make the arches. The players didn't wait their turns and quarrelled over their hedgehogs. The Queen stamped about, shouting, 'Off with his head!' or, 'Off with her head!' every few minutes.

Soon the game was over. All the players, except the King and Queen and Alice, had been sentenced to be beheaded. Alice was relieved to hear the King whisper to them, 'You are all pardoned.'

Alice was talking to the Duchess when a trumpet sounded in the distance.

'The trial's beginning! Come on!' said the Duchess, taking Alice by the hand.

WHO STOLE THE TARTS?

The courtroom was crowded, and the King and Queen of Hearts were sitting on their thrones.

Near the King stood the White Rabbit, with a trumpet in one hand and a parchment scroll in the other. The Knave of Hearts was in chains, standing between two soldiers.

On a table was a dish of tarts. (Alice hoped that they were the refreshments!)

There was a jury box with twelve creatures in it: animals, birds and a small lizard named Bill. They were all writing on slates. 'They're putting down their names, in case they forget them,' whispered the Duchess.

'Stupid things!' said Alice loudly.

'*SILENCE IN COURT!*' cried the White Rabbit. The jury were busy writing down 'Stupid things!'

'Herald! Read the accusation!' said the King sternly.

The White Rabbit blew three blasts on his trumpet, unrolled his scroll, and read:

'The Queen of Hearts, she made some tarts,
*   All on a summer's day.*
The Knave of Hearts, he stole those tarts,
*   And took them clean away.'*

'Consider your verdict!' cried the King.

'Not yet, your Majesty!' the White Rabbit hastily interrupted. 'The trial comes first!'

'Call the first witness!' said the King.

This was the Mad Hatter. He had a teacup in one hand and a piece of bread and butter in the other.

'You ought to have finished your tea by now,' said the King. 'When did you begin?'

'Fourteenth of March, I think,' said the Hatter.

'Fifteenth,' said the March Hare, who was also in the courtroom.

'Sixteenth,' said the Dormouse, who was sitting next to Alice.

'Write that down,' said the King. The jury eagerly wrote it down and added it up.

'Give your evidence and don't be nervous,' said the King, 'or I'll have you executed on the spot!'

While the Hatter was giving his evidence, the Dormouse complained to Alice, 'I wish you wouldn't squeeze me so!'

'I can't help it,' said Alice. 'I'm growing!'

'Then grow somewhere else,' grumbled the Dormouse.

'Call the next witness!' said the King.

Alice and the Dormouse looked up, just as the White Rabbit, in his shrill little voice, read out the name '*ALICE!*'

ALICE'S EVIDENCE

'Here!' cried Alice. She jumped up, forgetting how large she had grown, and knocked over the jury box. The jurors went sprawling into the crowd. Alice picked them up and put them back.

'What do you know about this business?' asked the King.

'Nothing!' said Alice.

Then the King read out, 'Rule Forty-two – all persons more than a mile high to leave the court.' Everyone looked at Alice.

'That's not a regular rule!' protested Alice. 'You've just invented it!'

'It's the oldest rule in the book!' said the King.

'Then it ought to be Number One!' said Alice.

'Consider your verdict,' said the King.

'No!' exclaimed the Queen. 'Sentence first, verdict after!'

'Stuff and nonsense!' cried Alice loudly. 'The *idea* of having the sentence first!'

'Hold your tongue!' bellowed the Queen.

'I won't!' said Alice.

'OFF WITH HER HEAD!' the Queen shouted at the top of her voice.

'Who cares for you?' said Alice. (She had grown to her full size by this time.) 'You're nothing but a pack of cards!'

At this, the whole pack rose up and came flying down on her. Alice gave a little scream, and tried to beat them off.

All at once she found herself lying on the grassy bank. Her sister was gently brushing away some of the dead leaves that had fluttered down from the tree onto Alice's face.

'Wake up, Alice dear!' she said. 'What a long sleep you've had!'